A Christmas Romance

IT STARTED WITH A SLEIGH

INTERNATIONAL BESTSELLING AUTHOR

KAYDENCE SNOW

It Started With A Sleigh

MORE BOOKS BY
KAYDENCE SNOW

THE EVELYN MAYNARD TRILOGY

Variant Lost

Vital Found

Vivid Avowed

Just Be Her

For Mariah Carey

THE SLEIGH

I turned the key in the ignition for the fourth time and patted the steering wheel, hoping to coax my shitbox of a car to life. The engine just made a pathetic metallic sound and gave up.

"No, no, no, baby. Come on." I turned the key again. The car *refused* to start.

With a growl, I banged my forehead against the steering wheel, cursing the rustbucket with words that would have made Santa blush. There was no way I'd be able to find a mechanic this late on Christmas Eve. I wouldn't be making it home. I was late for the family dinner as it was, but now I wouldn't even be able to get there in time for dessert. My mom's rum balls, my aunt's famous Baked Alaska ...

I turned to the presents piled in the back seat. I'd have to trudge up three flights of stairs to get them all back into my apartment—

after I'd carried them all down.

I sighed, and my breath made a puff, even inside the car. It still hadn't snowed, but for days now, it had felt like the fluffy stuff was about to come tumbling down at any moment.

At least lugging presents will keep me warm, I tried to tell myself, but my jaw clenched in anger, rebelling against my own attempt at positivity.

Christmas was my favorite time of year. Even working at a big department store hadn't killed my love of the holiday. It was supposed to be a time of peace, love, and generosity, but there was nothing quite like the pressure of gift giving to bring out the worst in humanity. In the weeks leading up to Christmas, I'd been yelled at, ignored, had things thrown at me, and been treated with disdain by customers, but I'd just gritted my teeth and looked up, across the sprawling department store, to find the tree. The giant, professionally decorated tree sat in the middle of the store, the shining star on top visible from anywhere. Anytime someone treated me like crap, I looked for the star and reminded myself to be cheerful.

How could I be upset when my manager had agreed to let me leave at five instead of making me stay until closing at midnight? I had pulled double Saturday shifts for weeks in exchange, but he'd still agreed, and it meant I could be home for dinner.

I'd raced back to my apartment—as much as I could when at the mercy of public transport—piled the gifts into my car, cued up my Christmas playlist, and ... and then the piece of shit had refused to start.

My phone went off. It was a text from my mom asking how far away I was and reminding me not to use my phone while driving. "The roads are icy, Sadie." I rolled my eyes. How did she not see the irony?

I took a deep breath and replied, letting her know I wouldn't be coming.

Within seconds, my phone exploded, every aunt, uncle, cousin, and family relation who'd no doubt just heard my mom announce my absence had something to say about it.

Every *ting* of a message made my eye twitch. I'd worked my ass off all year, never even asked for time off. All I wanted was to go home for Christmas Eve, and I couldn't even have *that*? What was the point? I was so done with making an effort, trying to smile through a season that made everyone stressed beyond words.

I put my phone on silent and tucked it into my pocket, resigned. Maybe I'd just get drunk on eggnog and watch *Miracle on 34th Street* for the thirty-fourth time.

Better yet, I'd get drunk on tequila, take down all the decorations, and watch a horror movie—something gory and gratuitous. How pathetic. Worst Christmas ever.

I banged my head against the steering wheel again. Simultaneously, a loud crash erupted from next to the building, accompanied by a bright light.

My head snapped up.

I rushed out of the car and ran around to the back parking area. There was no one around. While the city still buzzed with last-minute shoppers and people trying to get home, my apartment building was on the outskirts, and everyone was inside avoiding the biting cold.

A lone sedan drove past as I moved along a row of parked cars, more cautiously now.

At the back of the dingy parking lot, one of the dumpsters lay toppled on its side, trash spilling out; the other two had been knocked out of their spots. Something dark and shiny was wedged between them.

Halfway between me and the mess lay a person, on the ground, not moving.

With a gasp, I rushed forward.

I skidded to a stop and dropped down next to him, the cold ground biting into my knees even through my boots. There didn't appear to be any blood. The man's green velvet coat with white fur trim was pristine, his handsome face unmarked.

I reached out to check his pulse, but before my hand connected, he gasped and shot up into a sitting position.

I made a choked, startled sound and backed away.

"He's up!" another voice called from the direction of the dumpsters.

A second man in a green velvet coat, this one with red fur trim, stood near the mess with his hands on his hips. "And we've got company."

The man next to me groaned, and I placed a hand on his shoulder. "Are you all right? What happened?" I shot his friend a dirty look. Why wasn't he trying to help?

The man on the ground shook his head as if to clear it, then looked at me. I couldn't tell what color his eyes were in the dark, but I could've sworn I saw a glint of white sparkle in them as he smiled. "Never better."

A loud *clang* had us both turning back to his inconsiderate friend. Whatever was between the two dumpsters steamed, and a frustrated grunt sounded from behind it. Was that a car? Had they crashed into the dumpsters?

A third man walked out from behind the steaming vehicle, wiping his hands on a rag. *His* green velvet coat was trimmed with golden fur and open in the front, despite the cold.

"What do you mean company?" he practically growled, rubbing at a stubborn spot on his finger.

The man beside me leaned back and launched himself to his feet in a maneuver worthy of a gymnast, then brushed his hands on his coat. He reached a hand down to me with a wide grin. The murky streetlight made his short blond hair look like a halo.

Reflexively I took his hand, and he pulled me to my feet, then just held on to me as he walked back to his friends.

The inconsiderate one—with red trim on his coat, dark skin, and black hair—watched us in confusion. The third one—gold trim and red hair—scowled as he threw the rag aside.

"So, which one of you jerks shoved me?" the man still holding my hand in his big warm one asked, chuckling. "We don't exactly have time for this."

Gold-trim gave him a withering look and gestured to the dumpsters. "No one shoved you, Tin. We crashed."

"Ohhh. Shit." He dropped my hand to run his fingers through his hair, cringing.

We all turned to look at the mess next to the dumpsters.

Now that I was close enough, I could see it wasn't a car. It was sleek and shiny, dark green with black details, but it looked more like a sleigh than anything else—if Ferrari made sleighs.

Their green velvet coats looked handmade and expensive, with large hoods and intricate embroidery at the edges. My plain black puffy coat and knee-high black leather boots were positively dull in comparison. My favorite reindeer scarf usually brightened the ensemble, but I'd managed to lose it on the bus that morning.

I looked between the three similarly dressed men and the sleigh and laughed.

"OK, so I'm guessing you were on your way to some Christmas party and crashed, right? Someone have too much eggnog? Is that supposed to be Santa's sleigh?"

They stared at me and then all burst into laughter. Well, two of them burst into laughter. The one with his coat still open, giving me a glimpse of a tight white undershirt straining against toned muscles, chuckled and shook his head.

The black-haired one pulled out a tablet and started prodding it while Tin answered, "That's not Santa's sleigh. You're funny." He crossed his arms and watched me with amusement.

Despite myself, I chuckled. "Right. Of course. How silly of me."

"Everyone knows Santa's sleigh is red. Big guy should be in eastern Europe around this time." The one with the tablet checked his watch. "Heading to the Middle East, actually. This is going to put us behind schedule."

Tin cringed. "Max doesn't like to fall behind. Makes him anxious. And yeah, big guy's got his sleigh with him. This is our sleigh. Well, the one assigned to us. You know what I mean."

I looked between them, the frustration from earlier returning. I'd thought they were hurt and rushed over, and now they were cracking jokes while I froze my ass off. *Worst Christmas ever. I wouldn't be surprised if they tried to mug me.*

"Very funny." I rolled my eyes. "I was just trying to help. I thought you seriously hurt yourself, but obviously this is some massive prank. Congratulations, I'm the idiot. Have a nice life."

I turned to leave, my blonde ponytail whipping around and flicking me in the face, but a hand clamped around my wrist. Max held me in place, his other hand still clutching the tablet, as he gave me an intense, searching look. Just like with Tin, I could've sworn his eyes glinted, but the color this time was a brilliant red.

"Wait. You're telling me you're not from the Pole?" he demanded.

"Are you trying to insinuate I'm a stripper?" I yanked my arm out of his grip and propped my hands on my hips. It was one thing to crack annoying Christmas jokes, but now they were insulting me?

"Crap. This is worse than I thought." Max started tapping at his tablet furiously. "El, can you check the——"

"Already on it." The redhead was leaning over the smoking sleigh, fiddling around with something out of sight.

Tin just stared at me, wide-eyed.

Confusion warred with frustration inside me. I couldn't figure these guys out. Were they hurt and in trouble? Were they trying to goad me? Insult me? Now they were acting like *I* was the weird one.

Only curiosity kept me from trudging back up to my empty apartment to spend Christmas Eve alone.

El straightened and marched back over to us, something in his hand obscured by the gold fur on his coat. He came to a stop right in front of me. He was at least a foot taller than my five-two curvy frame and had to lean down to stare into my face. His eyes glinted too——the most mesmerizing gold.

He watched me but spoke to his buddies. "The mirage mech is shot. So's the flight system."

Max groaned. "What are we gonna do? We're only halfway through the deliveries."

I didn't look at him; I was too mesmerized by the gold in El's eyes. He had freckles across the bridge of his nose and on his cheeks. It would've been adorable if not for the relentless scowl he had pinned on me.

"We go old school." El held up a snow globe over his shoulder. "But I don't know how the hell this one's supposed to help. There's not a scrap of Christmas spirit coming off her."

He looked me up and down and finally stepped back.

I bristled and found my voice. "Hey, screw you, *Buddy the Elf*. I have plenty of Christmas spirit. I fucking *love* Christmas. It's just been a shitty day, between the ridiculously long hours at work where people treat me like scum, and losing my favorite scarf with the reindeer on it, and the coffee shop being out of mint flavor. Then to top it all off, my damn car won't start, so I can't go be with my family, and instead of consoling me, they're all sending me passive-aggressive texts to make me feel guilty about something that isn't even my fault!" I was yelling by the end, getting all my frustration with my disaster of a day out. I probably looked like as much of a nut as the three grown-ass men talking about sleighs and dressed as ...

"Wait a minute. What even are you supposed to be?"

"Elves," they said at the same time, and El rolled his eyes.

I rolled mine right back. "OK. Whatever." Once again, I turned to leave.

"Wait!" This time it was Tin who held me back, both his hands wrapped around my forearm. "You have to help us. Please!"

"I tried that. You cracked jokes, remember?" I shook him off.

"I was fine." He waved one hand in the air. "Elves can't get hurt at Christmas. There's a whole protection-magic thing."

"Ah, here we go," Max cut in. He stepped forward, the tablet in front of his face. "Sadie Harmony Purcell of Apartment 38, 1285 Benson Street."

A cold chill ran down my spine. How could he possibly know that? Was I in more trouble than I thought? I'd texted Mom—no one was expecting me anywhere for hours, maybe days. How long would it be before anyone realized I was missing? What if it snowed and my body wasn't discovered until spring?

Undeterred by the look of utter horror on my face, Max flashed me a grin. "Nice. For the most part. You were on the naughty list between the ages of sixteen and nineteen, but you've more than made up for it with six straight years on the nice list since then."

They were deranged. A group of hot, deranged Christmas murderers.

Max scrolled down. "Last year you wished for a sewing machine. The year before it was a good set of drawing pencils. The year before..."

El waved his hand in front of the tablet. "We don't have time for this. She's freaking out."

They all looked at me. My eyes were so wide they felt ready to pop out of my head. I hadn't even told anyone about the sewing machine. How could they *possibly* know that?

"Just skip to the year of disbelief." Tin nudged Max's shoulder, and he huffed before scrolling farther down.

"Let's see here … Stopped believing in Santa at age twelve. Wished for grandma to not have cancer anymore. Also wished for grandma to live to see Christmas. Due to limitations on granting longevity and immortality wishes, secondary wish was granted." He looked up at me with sad eyes. "Grandma lived through Christmas Day and passed away in her sleep that night."

Tin gripped my elbow gently. "I'm sorry about your grandma."

A single tear tracked a path down my cheek, and I swatted it away with numb, freezing fingers.

"I'm sorry too." El's voice was gentle, but his next words kind of ruined it. "But we really don't have time for this. We need to get moving if we're going to have a snowball's chance of doing our jobs tonight, and we need your help."

"This is real?" I had to hear them say it.

"Really real," Max confirmed as Tin nodded, still rubbing my elbow soothingly.

"Am I losing my mind?"

"No." El shrugged. "But a lot of kids are going to be sad and disappointed if we don't get our sleigh up and running before midnight."

"Wait. What does this have to do with me? Why do you need *my* help? I have no idea what's going on here."

Max tried to explain. "The manual reads that, in the event of a crash or other sleigh failure, an assistant will be assigned to facilitate whatever needs to be done to get us back in the air. This hasn't happened in the whole time we've been doing this. We just assumed the assistant would be someone from the North Pole, but the manual doesn't explicitly state that, so I guess you're it."

"I'm here so I'm it?" I raised an eyebrow, and he shrugged.

I groaned and crossed my arms. It wasn't as if I had anything better to do. "What exactly do you expect me to do?"

"We have to recharge the flux capacitor," El announced.

I frowned. "That's a real thing? Isn't that for time travel?"

He flashed the first genuine grin I'd seen on his face—he had dimples, dammit!—and they all laughed.

"Time travel's not real, silly." Tin shook his head as El pulled a black tarp out of the sleigh and draped it over the mess.

"Right. Of course. Flying sleighs and Christmas magic are totally legit, but time travel is laughable. Duh!" My tone dripped sarcasm. If this was how they were going to treat me, it would be a long night.

"We need to recharge the main power core so the sleigh can get all its functions up and running again," Max explained. El held up the snow globe again before tucking it in his pocket.

"How do we do that?" I asked as we started to walk across the parking lot.

Tin smiled at me. "Christmas cheer, of course!"

THE CAROLS

As we neared the end of the parking area, Max asked, "So, Sadie, do you have a car? Our ride is kind of out of commission."

I chuckled, then cringed. "Yeah, about that..."

We rounded the corner, and my heart sank as we approached the rustbucket, realization dawning.

"Oh no. Please, no, no, no." I leaned in. All the presents were gone. "Damn it!"

I slammed the door shut and kicked the tire for good measure, even though it wasn't the car's fault I'd stupidly left it wide open in a shady neighborhood.

"What's wrong?" Tin drew my attention back to my three new elf friends, all watching me with worried expressions.

"I left my car open in my rush to check on the crash, and all my presents have been stolen. This is the worst Christmas *ever*," I grumbled and leaned against the car, fighting back tears. Not only would I not be home in time to see my family, but when I did finally get there, I'd be empty-handed.

"Uh, I'm gonna need you to rein in the Grinch attitude." El shook the snow globe in front of my face. It was an old-fashioned one, with an intricate gold base and a winter scene with a cottage and Christmas trees, but everything was kind of gray, the water murky. It looked dull and flat, despite the level of detail and craftsmanship in the base. "We're supposed to be recharging this, not draining it further."

"Elvis, don't be an asshole," Tin scolded him.

Max rubbed the back of his black hair. "I'm sorry about your presents, Sadie, but we are on a tight schedule."

Tin stepped in front of me, blocking the other two from my view, and grabbed my hands. "Ignore them." He pulled me away from the car and into a hug.

I stiffened for a moment—he was a total stranger—but his strong arms held me tightly around the middle, and he rocked me from side to side, and he smelled amazing! Like mint and an open fire—fresh and comforting at the same time. It made me think of curling up by a roaring fire, a decorated tree in the corner and a mint hot chocolate in my hands while Nat King Cole crooned about a white Christmas.

Before I knew it, I'd relaxed into the hug and closed my eyes, resting my cheek on the soft velvet covering his shoulder.

"Wait." My eyes snapped open, and I pulled out of the embrace to turn on the other two. "Elvis?"

The redheaded elf crossed his arms. "El is short for Elvis."

"So…" I giggled, my warm breath making puffs in the cold air. "You're Elvis the elf?"

"Yes. My name is Elvis and I'm an elf. Can we please get on with it?"

Tin and I burst out laughing, and even Max pressed his lips together, visibly holding in his mirth.

Elvis threw his hands up. "My mother was a fan, OK?"

"Yeah, but we do get to pick our elf names, and you chose to stick with it," Max pointed out, then gestured at Tin. "Meanwhile, this one just assumed you couldn't keep your given name."

I turned to Tin with a grin. "What is it?"

He grinned back, not at all bothered by the teasing. "My given name is Timothy, and yeah, I thought we had to pick a Christmassy elf name, so I picked Tinsel. Tim, Tin"— he shrugged—"close enough."

I laughed and turned to Max, raising a questioning brow.

"My given and elf name is Max—short for Maxwell."

"Oh." My shoulders drooped. That wasn't nearly as fun as the other two.

"Now, is this your car?" With names out of the way, Max was determined to get us moving.

"Yep, and it's a shitbox that won't start. Sorry, boys, but I guess we're walking."

They all groaned and huffed.

"Wait. Where exactly are you guys taking me? Where are we supposed to go?"

"This neighborhood isn't particularly … cheerful." El looked around at the plain brick buildings, hardly a decoration in sight. A dog barked in the distance. "I'm sure plenty of these apartments have decorations up and they're doing Christmas Eve things, but we can't exactly barge into people's homes. And that wouldn't be enough juice anyway. We need a crowd."

Max whipped out his tablet. "According to the manual, for the power core to recharge, it needs to be in the proximity of people experiencing the 'holiday spirit.' It is recommended to seek out larger groups, as this fosters greater spreading of said spirit. Depending on current location, it is suggested we immerse ourselves in the local holiday customs and traditions. Gathering Christmas-related items in order to boost the signal and maintain the charge is also recommended. Once again, these items will be specific to region and customs and may include, but are not limited to, plant materials such as Christmas trees (pine, spruce, fir, etc.), holly, frankincense, myrrh, poinsettias..." He trailed off, scrolled, then picked up the list once more. "Food stuffs, such as gingerbread cookies, fruit mince pies, eggnog, mulled wine..." He scrolled again. "Decorative and seasonal items, such as baubles, lights, candles, wreaths, ornamental—"

"OK, we get the picture," Tin interrupted and nudged me with a shoulder. "We just gotta find some people getting their Christmas on."

What was within walking distance and Christmassy enough to satisfy them? I thought for a moment, then snapped my fingers. "We'll go to the park. There's a Christmas concert on—people singing along to carols, waving candles and stuff. And it's only a fifteen-minute walk."

Max smiled. "Perfect. Lead the way."

I nodded and took off down the street.

Tin fell into step next to me. "The best way to spread Christmas cheer is singing loud for all to hear." He grinned. "Nice one, Sadie. I knew you could do it."

"Did you just quote that elf movie?"

"It's my favorite movie."

I laughed and leaned against him, wrapping my arm around his as we walked. Ever since he'd hugged me, I just wanted to snuggle back into him, breathe in his comforting smell.

"He says that about all holiday movies," El interjected.

"And songs," Max added.

The temperature only continued to drop, but the walk was warming me up, and despite its boring black color, my puffy coat was pretty warm. My one good pair of black boots kept me steady on the icy ground.

As we passed through the park's main gate, the soft sound of voices singing in chorus reached us. El pulled out the snow globe and smiled. Some of the snow inside was beginning to swirl, and the little cottage suddenly looked as if it had a candle flickering in the window.

He rushed ahead down the path, Max hot on his heels, while Tin and I jogged to catch up.

The park's main lawn came into view once we rounded the bend. On a stage at the bottom of a hill, an orchestra and a woman in a stunning red gown were halfway through "Silent Night." People huddled together on picnic blankets and folding chairs, steaming cups clutched in mittened hands as they sang along. Some of them waved candles while children in Santa hats ran and played among the crowd.

We moved to the edge of the audience, and the guys all sat down on the cold ground. Tin pulled me down into the spot between him and Max.

I made sure my coat was under my butt and tightened my plain red scarf. "So, what do we do now?"

"We enjoy the music and give the power core time to soak it in," Max answered, his eyes on the stage.

After the frantic, worried way they'd been carrying on earlier, I was surprised by how calm they all were. They just sat there, mouthing the words to every single song. One by one, they pulled their fur-lined hoods up to ward off the cold. Now that we were no longer on the move, my fingers and toes were getting chilly. I pulled the sleeves of my coat down over my knuckles, kicking myself for leaving my gloves in the car.

Tin scooted over until he was pressed up against my side and took my hands in his, giving them a rub.

"Why are your hands so warm?" I sighed.

He smiled and shrugged. "I think it's a Christmas-magic thing. We're kept protected and safe from pretty much everything during the drop time."

Before I could ask more, Max scooted over on my other side, boxing me in against Tin.

"Are you cold?" he asked.

"It's freezing. Just because you guys can't feel it doesn't mean I can't."

He frowned. "We can't have you getting sick." He looked around, as if to check if anyone was watching, then leaned into me, hunching his shoulders around his hands.

Glittering red shimmer appeared over his palm, materializing out of nothing, and I gasped. It swirled around for a moment and then faded, leaving behind a large mug with a cartoon Santa on it. He held it out to me. "You like mint in your hot chocolate, right?"

"How did you…" I took the hot drink from him, dazed.

Tin draped an arm over my shoulders as I sipped on the best hot chocolate I'd ever tasted. As a choir filed onto the stage, the drink warmed me from the inside out, almost as comforting as Tin's arm around me.

"Don't tell him I said so, but this is even better than my dad's hot chocolate." I took another sip but paused when I felt Max stiffen against my side.

"We're keeping you from your family," he said as they all gave me serious looks. "Maybe we can do this without her, guys."

They made to get up, but I waved them down. "Relax. It's my shitty car keeping me from my family. It had broken down before you guys crashed. I've already messaged my mom and told her I'm not gonna make it. I have a million passive-aggressive texts to prove it."

They settled back down but watched me suspiciously.

El leaned around Max. "So you were on your way to your parents'? That's what all the presents were for?"

"Yeah." I sighed. "I worked so much overtime this past month so my boss would let me out at five. I still wasn't going to make it to my parents' place before dinner, but I would've been there for dessert, and I could've spent time with my family, woken up with them on Christmas morning. This is the third year I'll be missing out. It sucks, because I really love Christmas." I pouted.

"Third year?" Tin asked.

"Yeah. I had to work until midnight the past two years. No way was I going to drive for two hours after such a long shift on icy roads.

It's made for lonely holidays the past few years. But at least I had my friend Monica to spend it with." Monica elected to avoid her family at Christmas, declaring they were all a bunch of assholes.

"Why do you live so far away from your family?"

"Can't you just take the whole day off?"

"Why can't you get there by public transport or something? You can still make it."

They all fired questions at me. They were being kind of intense about it, but I guessed it came with the territory.

"Whoa." I laughed and took another sip of my delicious drink. "They live way past the end of the train line, and the last bus left hours ago. There's no one else to drive me, so I'm stuck. My home town is great, really cozy and friendly, but I moved to the city for work. And there is no such thing as days off during December when you work in retail. I was lucky to get even the evening off."

"Do you see your family often?" El asked.

"As much as I can. But living in the city is not cheap, and the minimum two-hour drive is a pain."

"Do you like your job?" Max asked.

"What's with the inquisition?" I chuckled but answered anyway. "I don't love it. But I have to work, and it's as close as I can get to what I actually want to be doing, so..."

"What do you want to be doing?" Tin asked.

"Um..." I finished the last of the hot chocolate to buy myself time. Why is it so hard to talk about what we truly want out of life? As if voicing it will make it real, put it out in the universe, and then if you fail, everyone will know. "I want to be a designer."

"Like an architect?" El cocked his head, the gold fur obscuring his eyes.

I shook my head and just said it. "Fashion. Undergarments specifically. I want to design lingerie."

Everyone was silent for a beat as the music reached a crescendo.

Then Tin smirked. "I bet your boyfriend loves that."

I leaned in, keeping my voice low and teasing like his. "I'm single."

"Excellent!" He kept staring at me as I breathed in his mint-and-woodsmoke scent and sighed.

"What?" Max leaned in, interrupting the moment. "We can't hear you."

"Sadie was just saying she doesn't have a boyfriend," Tin supplied helpfully.

"Oh, great! I mean cool. I mean, yeah, OK, uh..." If he hadn't been literally pressed up against my side, I wouldn't have noticed the slight flush creeping up Max's dark cheeks.

El just laughed softly, looking between the three of us. When my eyes met his, he very purposefully glanced down my body. My puffy coat ensured he couldn't see much of anything, but the deliberate look made it clear he was wondering what was under there.

If the hot chocolate and the man sandwich weren't enough to warm me up, the interest from three gorgeous men did the job, and I suddenly felt a bit hot.

Were they even allowed to date humans? Or did they have to stick to elves to keep the secret? Was interspecies romance allowed in the North Pole? What even were they? They clearly weren't the cute, short version of elves I'd had in my mind all my life.

I never in my wildest dreams thought I'd be sitting in a park on Christmas Eve wondering about my sexual attraction to a damn Santa's elf! But there I was, with three of the tallest, strongest, most caring, sexy elves I could've ever imagined.

If it wasn't for the cold ground making my ass go numb, I would've assumed I'd had too much eggnog at my parents' and had already passed out on the couch.

THE ELVES

Since they'd thrown question after question at me, I figured it was only fair to throw some right back at them. Plus, I needed to get off the topic of my single status. I'd broken up with my ex Brian six months ago. I was pretty much over him, but his accounting firm was a block away from where I worked, and I kept bumping into him, making it all come up again. I really wasn't in the mood to rehash that mess.

"So, how does this all work exactly?"

Max frowned. "How does what work?"

I waved around at the three of them. "This Christmas-magic, delivering-presents, Santa-is-real situation. I mean, I gotta be honest, when I thought about elves, I did not picture ... this."

"And what exactly is *this*?" There was a teasing glint in Tin's eyes.

I gave him a disparaging look. "You all know you're hot. Stop deflecting and tell me about Santa."

They laughed, but Max took pity on me. "Santa used to do it all himself. But that was millennia ago. The world's population was nowhere near what it is now. The traditions were different. As the population grew, so did his team. He makes an appearance on every continent and delivers as many presents as he can himself, but we do the rest."

"The three of you? Do we have time to be watching a Christmas concert?"

"Nah, we're just one team." He waved me down. "There are thousands of elves now. We each get assigned a region every year—a certain portion of the population."

"Are all elves dudes? Seems a bit sexist."

"Nope," El piped in. "Fifty-fifty, and we have pay transparency—no gender pay gap in the North Pole. That's really important to Mr. and Mrs. Claus."

"Right. Of course. How silly of me to assume." I couldn't help laughing. Half the things they were saying were making me giggle, either because they were so unexpected or just because these guys were funny. Witty even.

"OK, but even with dividing the world into sections, how do you get it all done? That's still millions of presents."

"Magic," Max whispered and pointed to my now empty mug.

I resisted smacking myself on the forehead. I kept expecting clear, logical answers to all my questions, but I was sitting at a Christmas concert with three actual elves from the North Pole. Of course there would be some magic involved.

"Some things don't need to be questioned. Some things just are. Not everything has to be controlled and understood. We're not meant to know it all, and that's OK." Tin squeezed my shoulder.

"I get that. I can't promise I'll stop asking questions though. This is pretty crazy for me."

"Long as you understand we won't always have answers."

I nodded.

"I like your coat." A tiny, sweet voice drew our attention to a little girl standing in front of Elvis. She was around five years old and bundled in swathes of red-and-white fabric.

"Uh ... thanks." El fiddled with the golden fur on one of his sleeves. I stifled a laugh.

"Can I touch it?" the child asked, clasping her mittened hands in front of herself.

"Um..." He looked over at us, like a deer in headlights. "I guess?"

She squealed and ripped her mitten off, bounding forward on little legs to grab a handful of the golden fur.

"It's so soft." She giggled.

"Look, this one's red, like your coat." I held Max's arm out for the little cutie, and she shuffled over to stroke his coat too. I couldn't blame her. Their coats were ridiculously soft and looked impressive.

"Maggie!" Two little boys—clearly her brothers—came running up. "Stop running off!" the older one chided her, but the younger boy just joined his little sister in petting Max's fur trim.

"Are you guys from the North Pole?" He wiped his runny nose on the back of his sleeve.

"We sure are!" Tin grinned as more kids wandered over to gawk at the overgrown Christmas elves.

"Should he be telling them that?" I whispered to Max.

He shrugged. "They're just kids, and it's Christmas Eve. What's the harm?"

The growing crowd of little, adorable people began firing off questions.

"Have you met Santa?"

"Do you have a reindeer?"

"Can I sit on your lap?"

"How come you're here and not helping Santa?"

Elvis remained mostly silent but let himself be poked and prodded by tiny hands wanting to touch his coat. Max and Tin answered the kids' questions and painted a vivid picture of life in the North Pole. The kids were enamored, and I couldn't stop grinning. It was the most adorable thing I'd ever seen.

A group dressed as elves—much less convincing than the guys—skipped out onto the stage and started to sing "Jingle Bells."

I got an idea and whispered it into Tin's ear.

He gave me a wide grin and a kiss on the cheek before leaning forward to get all the kids' attention. "Hey, who likes this song?"

"Me, me, me!" all the kids yelled over one another.

"Who wants to see something cool?"

Another chorus of "me, me, me."

Tin looked around exaggeratedly, then rubbed his hands together and held them out palms up.

Sparkly white magic swirled over his hands, just like the red magic had when Max conjured my hot chocolate. The kids all gasped and stared, transfixed. The magic twisted and molded into the shape of a little sleigh pulled by reindeer. It shot out of Tin's hands to go sailing past all the delighted little faces, then faded.

They all clapped and demanded more, launching into questions about reindeer.

I leaned back on my hands, and El's pocket immediately drew my attention. The snow globe glowed and then faded. He glanced down at it too, then his eyes met mine behind Max's back. He gave me a genuine smile and nodded.

There is no joy in the world purer than that of a child. Those kids were loving every second of the Christmas magic the elves' stories and showing off were bringing them, and the power core was juicing up.

Max made a show of rubbing his hands together, declaring he wouldn't be outdone by Tin's sleigh display, as I wrapped my arms around my knees. The temperature was continuing to drop.

Tin sprang to his feet and held a hand out to me. "Come on. A walk will warm you up."

I let him pull me up, and we wandered away from the crowd and down the path, the music and laughter fading behind us.

"I'm not sure we should've left those two on their own." I laughed.

"Yeah, El has no idea how to handle kids." Tin chuckled. "But Max has it covered. They'll be fine."

"So ... did you grow up at the North Pole or ... ?" I wasn't sure how to broach the subject. They were so different from my idea of elves, and they seemed to know how the regular world worked. I couldn't figure them out.

He laughed again. I loved his laugh—it was musical and carefree but still deep and masculine, and it came freely and easily, as if he found joy just about everywhere.

"No, I was born in Saint Louis."

"Oh." I frowned. "OK, I'm confused. How did you end up driving a sleigh?"

"I don't drive. El drives and maintains it. Max keeps everything organized—checks the list twice and all that. I'm the delivery man. Also, I'm in charge of snacks."

"You know what I mean." I smacked him lightly on the chest. He captured my hand and threaded his fingers through mine.

"OK, fine. I'll tell you. So, you know that Santa's setup had to expand as the population grew, but at the start it was just him and the Elves—capital E. They're incredible magical creatures and pretty much immortal—much closer to the short-statured, pointy-eared types you imagined. We're like ... extended, adopted family. Something like a cross between family and valued employees. The Elves have immense power, and now they mostly help the Clauses run the Pole and manage the operation. We only have limited magic, and we only have access to it at Christmastime to do our jobs."

"But you're all elves? How does that work?"

"Kind of." He tilted his head from side to side. "The title has more meaning in the Pole. Like, Shinny Upatree is one of Santa's original helpers. She's an Elf with a capital *E*. Elvis, Max, and I were recruited. We're elves with a lowercase *e*. Pole politics can get a little complicated, but it's really wonderful most of the time."

"Wait. Recruited?" I paused to look at him, but he tugged me along. The path had gotten narrow, and the trees were denser in this part of the park. Most were pines, rising high into the inky sky. If it had snowed, it would've been the perfect Christmas scene.

"Yeah. I had no idea any of this was real until an Elf with a capital *E* showed up and asked if I wanted a job, an adventure, and a family wrapped into one."

"Did you think you were losing your mind? I thought I was when you all started doing magic and Max knew personal details about me."

"Yeah ... for about five seconds. Then I was all in." He shrugged.

"Just like that? They must've made you one hell of an offer," I joked, but Tin only stared at the ground, suddenly serious. Silence settled between us, and our misted breath mingled.

"Did I say something wrong? I'm sorry." I squeezed his warm hand, and he gave mine a squeeze back.

"No, not at all. I just ... you'd be with your family right now, yeah? If your car hadn't broken down, you'd be spending the holidays with them? Enjoying their company, eating food, sharing traditions?"

"Yeah..." I frowned, confused at the sudden change of topic.

"See, there's something the guys and I have in common—all recruited elves do. We've got no one to miss us at Christmas."

My heart cracked—a hairline fracture invisible to the eye but just as painful as if it had shattered into pieces for all to see. I didn't know what to say.

"I don't know who my birth parents are. I was left at the front doors of a firehouse at six weeks old. Medical tests revealed I had a heart condition—hypoplastic left heart syndrome, or HLHS. Say that three times quickly! Haha! Anyway, it made adoption pretty much impossible. No one wanted to take on a baby with so many complicated health problems. It all worked out in the end—with a couple of operations and medication I was fine, but by then it was too late. No one wants to adopt a ten-year-old."

I pulled him to a stop and held his hand in both of mine. He kept his gaze on the trees as he spoke, his thumb trailing rhythmic circles on the back of my hand.

"All my life, since I was old enough to understand the concept of Santa, I wished for the same thing every year…"

"Family," we both whispered, and the fracture in my heart cracked a little wider.

"Even after I stopped believing in Santa, I still wished for family. But I was always a happy kid. I loved Christmas, and I was always the first one to volunteer to help decorate whichever home or state-run institution I was living in. I did activities with the younger kids, I sang carols, I helped the staff wrap presents. I was all over it.

"So, when an honest-to-God Elf appeared in my room in the share house I was living in with a bunch of other twenty-somethings trying to finish college, you bet your ass I dropped it all and said yes before I even knew what the full offer was."

He looked back down the dark, winding path. The lights of the performance glowed over the tops of the pine trees. "They're my family now. Elvis and Maxwell are my brothers, and we take care of each other no matter what."

"That's a heartbreaking story, Tin." I coughed to beat back the lump in my throat as I leaned up to hug him, wrapping my arms tightly around his neck.

He hugged me back but chuckled. "What are you talking about? It has a happy ending. Santa granted my wish. I may have had a rough start in life, but I have a family now, and I get to spend every Christmas bringing joy to people all over the world. I'm happy, Sadie. I was just trying to explain how people from the real world end up crashing out of the sky in a sleigh."

I leaned back but kept my hands on his shoulders. He rested his on my hips.

"So, all elves are like that? They don't have anyone who'll miss them on Christmas Eve?"

"We're not all orphans, but yeah, in a nutshell."

So, they all had stories to tell. I wanted to know Max's and El's too. I wanted to know more about them all and how they'd ended up crashing at my feet.

I pushed Tin's hood back to see his face properly, running my fingers through the soft white fur. His blond hair was falling in a wavy mess over his forehead, and I brushed it away. It was softer than the fur trim.

His arms circled my back and drew me closer, that glint of white sparkling in his green eyes. His full lips were parted, his breath misting in the cold. I closed my eyes and leaned in. My lips brushed his in a soft, barely there kiss.

A twig snapped in the trees to my right. My eyes widened as I startled in Tin's arms, breaking the kiss before it had really started.

We both turned to scan the trees as best we could in the dark.

Another twig snapped, followed by rustling. I frowned. Whatever it was sounded big. My heart started to beat a little faster as my mind offered picture after picture of feral wild animals.

I shuffled my feet, ready to run, but Tin's strong arms kept me in place.

The branches rustled again, followed by a grunting sound mixed with a loud exhale.

Whatever was stalking us was *huge*.

THE REINDEER

For the second time that night, I wondered how long it would be before they discovered my body. Would it even be recognizable? What the hell was I thinking wandering into the dark woods at night with a guy I'd only just met?

I chanced looking away from the ominous, rustling darkness to glance back at Tin's face, just in time to see it break into a massive grin. I hadn't even realized how tense his shoulders were until they relaxed, his arms around me loosening.

He looked down at me and took a step back, the smile never wavering.

"Come on." He grabbed my hand and pulled me in the direction of the beast.

I planted my feet and tried to yank him back. "What, are you crazy? We need to get the fuck out of here."

"Oh, no, it's OK. He's not gonna hurt you. Come on." He gave me a reassuring smile and another tug but didn't try to drag me unwilling into the scary situation. He just patiently waited.

I eyed the darkness, and the rustling and grunting started up again. I looked back into Tin's eyes. There wasn't even a hint of fear. If anything, he looked kind of excited.

"Is this the part where you feed me to some kind of evil beast as a sacrifice to get your sleigh moving again?"

He threw his head back and laughed. "No one's seen a Krampus in years. I promise no one is going to hurt you. I've got you, Sadie."

"What's back there?" I chewed on my lip, unsure. His complete lack of fear was putting me at ease somewhat, but I was still wary.

"Just let me show you. Trust me?"

After another few glances between the darkness and my new elf friend, I finally nodded. Immediately, he led the way through the pines, carefully stepping over the frozen ground and ducking under low-hanging limbs. We emerged into a small clearing, the moon peeking through the thick branches to illuminate the area.

In the middle stood a reindeer.

My eyes widened, this time in awe more than fear, and I froze, clutching Tin's hand again. The reindeer was huge; its antlers looked deadly, but at least it wasn't charging. It was just standing there, eyeing us. I didn't think this park had any wildlife bigger than racoons.

"Those antlers look like they could take out a pro wrestler. Maybe we should just leave?" I eyed Tin out of the corner of my eye, keeping my focus on the magnificent beast. It shuffled in place and made that grunting noise I'd heard in the dark. It almost sounded offended that I'd insinuated it would try to hurt us.

Tin just shrugged and moved forward, dragging me along with him. "Any other time of the year, I'd agree with you. But at Christmastime, we have a certain understanding with the reindeer. It's rare, but when elves have to spend a bit of time in the real world during Christmas, creatures like reindeer tend to be drawn to us. Our sleighs are powered by a more modern kind of magic these days, but there is a reason the cliché of Santa's sleigh being pulled by flying reindeer is a cliché. Once upon a time, this guy's ancestor probably helped Santa get his work done."

The reindeer let us walk right up to it, close enough that I could see my reflection in its dark eye. He made another kind of grunting sound and snorted out a breath, but he kept pretty still, even when Tin patted him on the nose.

Bit by bit, the fear left me, the magic of the situation bringing out giddy excitement to replace the adrenaline. I reached out a tentative hand and patted the reindeer's neck. He was soft and warm under my palm, and it almost felt like he leaned into my touch.

I shared a wide smile with Tin as we petted the magnificent animal in the moonlight.

After a few moments, the reindeer shook his head from side to side, making us duck out of the way of his powerful antlers. We stepped back, and it lowered its head in something resembling a bow. Tin gave it a slow nod back, and the reindeer turned and walked off into the trees, disappearing into the darkness.

I turned to Tin, a huge grin on my face. "That..." I whispered and punctuated every word with a nod. "Was. Freaking. Awesome."

"I told you to trust me." He smiled and came to stand directly before me. "Now, where were we before we were rudely interrupted by Prancer?"

"That was *Prancer?*"

He wrapped his arms around my waist. "You're missing the point," he whispered against my lips as he started to walk me backward.

"What's the point?" I threaded my fingers through the hair at the back of his head as my back connected with a pine tree.

"This," he breathed before pressing his lips against mine. His weight pinned me to the tree as his tongue teased my lips. I opened for him, deepening the kiss.

I dragged my hands around from his neck to the top of his chest and pushed gently. He pulled his mouth away from mine and watched me, breathing hard.

"Shouldn't we be ... you know ... collecting x-mas juice or whatever, to power the sleigh?" My brain wasn't working properly, and my breathy voice was just short of a moan.

Tin flashed me his perfect teeth. "There's more than one way to feel ... cheerful."

He pressed his hips forward, and his arousal dug into my belly. My breath hitched, heat pooling between my thighs.

"Next you're gonna tell me to jingle your bells," I teased.

"If that's what you're into." He pushed a knee between my legs and rocked his hips. I rolled mine, desperately seeking friction.

"You're sure we have time for this?" I really hoped he wouldn't say no, but I couldn't be responsible for kids not getting their presents just because I was horny. I couldn't have that on my conscience.

He nodded. "Positive."

"In that case..."

I pushed against his chest, more forcefully now, until he backed up and I was able to switch places with him. With a grin on his face, he let me maneuver him so he was leaning back against the tree.

I plastered my front against his and kissed him again. He trailed his hands down to grip my ass through my bulky coat.

I was no longer cold. It was clearly still freezing, our uneven breaths misting in the air, but I couldn't feel it. With my heart hammering and my arousal sending heat down my spine to the spot between my legs, I was positively *hot*. And there was way too much clothing between us.

I broke the kiss and started kissing and licking Tin's jaw. His minty, smoky smell was both exciting and comforting at once. He smelled so good I wanted to lick him—so I did. I licked and nipped his neck as I popped the ornate buttons on his coat one after another. His skin was pale in the moonlight and hot and smooth under my mouth.

With the last button undone, I opened his coat and ran my hand down his front. He wore black pants and a plain white T-shirt—just like the one that had peeked out of El's open coat earlier. And just like El's, it clung to his body. His chest and stomach were hard under my touch. I lifted the hem of the T-shirt just enough to snake my fingers underneath, to feel the soft hair disappearing under his belt, the smooth muscle as it clenched under my cold fingers.

In a fraction of the time it had taken me to unbutton his coat, Tin pulled my zipper down and wrapped his arms around my waist under the puffy fabric. Without even glancing down at what I looked like under there, he pulled me up against him and kissed me hard. His hand roamed my body as his mouth explored mine.

I moaned and started to writhe against him, spreading my legs, seeking friction. His rock-hard erection pressed against my front, but I needed it just a little lower.

With a strong arm around my back and his tongue still down my throat, Tin reached down with his free hand and pulled my leg up until it was hitched over his hip. He bent his knees slightly, and suddenly his hardness was exactly where I wanted it. I gasped and rolled my hips against his. He kissed my neck and dragged his hand up the outside of my thigh. As we ground against each other, he grabbed my ass under my dress and kneaded the flesh, his strong grip pushing me harder against his gyrating hips.

I threw my head back to give him better access to my throat, and he sucked at that sensitive spot in the curve, making me moan into the darkness. With only one foot planted on the ground, I was glad he was holding me so tightly.

I'd never had sex outside, certainly never considered it when the smell of snow was in the air, but I figured there was a first time for everything.

The thrill of getting caught only made me more aroused; moisture pooled at my core as I smiled and dropped my head to kiss him again.

He grunted, and the hand at my back moved down to join his other hand on my ass.

Resting my knee on the rough bark of the tree for balance, I pulled back a fraction. He whimpered at the sudden lack of friction and opened his eyes. That glint of white magic sparked in them again, rendering me momentarily mesmerized, but I shook it off and wedged my arms between us. I held his gaze, both of us breathing heavily, as I undid his pants and pulled back the elastic of his underwear until I could put my hand down there.

I gripped him by the base and stroked up, caressing the tip with my thumb. He sighed and his eyes drooped, but he kept them open, kept watching me. I bit my bottom lip as I stroked him again, and he panted, his swollen lips parted.

Voices and the approaching crunch of leaves made my hand pause halfway down Tin's erection. My eyes widened.

He twitched in my hand as his mouth quirked up in an almost smile.

"It's just El and Max," he whispered inches from my mouth. "They won't mind. They'll wait for us to finish ... or join in, if you want them to."

I didn't think my eyes could widen any farther, but they did. I had no idea what to say to that. My body flushed, some part of me clearly liking the idea—I was attracted to all three of them. I just didn't know what to make of Tin's blasé attitude to the idea of group sex.

The two elves in question entered the little clearing.

"There you are," El announced as Max gasped and cursed. "Shit. Sorry. Uh..."

"And that's why you've been gone so long." There was amusement in El's voice.

I kept my back to them as I extracted my hand from Tin's pants, stepped away, and fumbled to zip up my coat.

"Please don't be embarrassed." Tin tilted his head to look into my eyes as he straightened his clothes and buttoned everything back up.

"I'm not." *Lies.* I was a little embarrassed. Intrigued as I was by Tin's insinuation, I'd never actually had an audience. "I'm just … uh, what did you mean about them joining in? Are you guys closer than I thought?"

Determined to handle this like an adult, I turned to face them all.

Max had his hands in his pockets, avoiding my eye. El was staring right at me with a hint of curiosity in his face.

Tin chuckled. "Nah. We're tighter than most families, but we didn't grow up together, so our bond is a little different. We kind of share everything."

"What?"

"Women," El stated, still looking at me steadily. "We share women from time to time. No, we don't have sex with each other, but we're not shy about putting a woman between us and seeing where it goes."

I thanked the Christmas spirits it was so damn cold—hopefully it would keep the blush from my face.

I cleared my throat. "Anyway, did you get enough charge or whatever to power your sleigh?"

They took pity on me and let me change the subject.

"No." Max finally joined the conversation. "The concert is wrapping up, and most of the parents are taking their kids home to warm beds. That was a great idea, by the way, Sadie—getting the kids involved."

I smiled. "Thanks."

Tin grabbed the bough of a nearby pine tree and yanked a bit off it. "Christmas tree." He held it up for the others to see. "And we had a visit from a reindeer." In his other hand, he produced a tuft of fur.

"Nice!" Max moved forward, extracting a black pouch from inside his coat, and Tin dropped the items into it.

"I got one of the programs from the concert—has all the carols listed with lyrics." Max added it to the pouch.

El joined our little circle and held up a tiny mitten with a snowflake embroidered on the back. We all turned to look at him.

"You stole a child's mitten? It's freezing," I admonished.

He raised a brow and pursed his lips. "The child was long gone. I found it abandoned on the ground as we left to look for you two."

He dropped the mitten into the pouch, and Max disappeared it back into his coat.

"OK, so what now?" I asked.

El took the snow globe out of his pocket. Once again, it was a little more alive than last time. The trees in the forest scene looked thicker and more detailed; the snow was swirling a little higher.

"We need more." El sighed and put it away again.

"How will you know when you have enough?"

"We'll just know," they chorused.

"OK then. So, what do we do now? Back to catch the rest of the concert?"

"Nah. No point. We got what we could from it, and all these Christmas trees helped." Max looked around. It really was beautiful out there. Peaceful.

"What else is close by? We need another Christmas crowd. More cheer." Tin leaned into me and grinned, reminding me of the cheer we'd very nearly shared just moments before.

I sighed. "We really need to get into the city, but without a car ...

Public transport? But a train will take forever."

We fell into silence as we started walking back toward the main gate.

I pulled out my cell phone. A taxi or an Uber would be crazy expensive, but maybe it was worth it. I checked both apps, only to groan at the expected wait times.

"Where to now?" Max asked, and three expectant elves stared at me.

"Uh..." I looked around, panic rising. Then an idea blossomed. "Actually, one of my friends lives two blocks that way." I pointed across the street. Cars were pulling away from the park, people spilling out through the gates now that the concert was over. "I know she's planning to head to a party in the city. Maybe she can give us a lift."

"Great!" Tin clapped. "I love parties."

"It's worth a try." El took the lead, setting a fast pace.

I checked the time—it was just before eight. Monica didn't usually leave for parties until well after ten, but this was her work's annual party, and they tended to start earlier. Hopefully we wouldn't be too late.

I sent her a quick text and caught up with El, matching his hurried steps even though my legs were way shorter than his.

THE EGGNOG

Monica was waiting on the sidewalk outside her apartment building when we rounded the corner. She'd replied to my text with a simple "OK" and hadn't asked any questions, but judging by the look on her face, she was about to ask them all now.

"Girl, I thought you'd be halfway to your folks' place by now. What the fuck happened?" She had her hands on her hips, pushing her open coat out to reveal the green sequined dress underneath. With her short black hair and killer stiletto boots, she looked stunning.

"That was the plan." I huffed, a little out of breath from keeping up with three sets of long legs and boundless energy. "But my car wouldn't start. Piece of shit."

She gave me a sympathetic look and drew me into a hug. When she pulled away, her eyes were on the three men behind me, her eyebrows raised. "And who are they?"

"Uh..." I glanced over my shoulder. Max had told me not to say anything to anyone about who they really were—it was against the rules unless the Christmas magic revealed them naturally, as it had to me. "They broke down right next to me. I figured if I couldn't get home to my family, at least I could help them out. We're trying to get into the city so they can get ... uh..."

"We need a part for the engine." Max smiled and stepped forward, extending his hand. "I'm Max. That's El and Tin."

El raised a half-hearted hand in greeting, his smile barely there. Tin grinned and waved enthusiastically. I held in a laugh at the polar-opposite reactions. So them ...

Monica shook Max's hand, but her eyes narrowed. "I don't think any mechanics are open, even in the city."

"Oh, we don't need a mechanic. The part is electrical. Any department store or, like, a Radio Shack or something will do."

"Right!" I spoke over Max. "Which is why we need to get there before everything closes. Can you give us a lift?"

"My car's in the garage, but you'll never find parking downtown." Monica waved her hand, but before my heart sank, she grinned and pointed to a black stretch limo pulling up at the street. "But I can give you a lift. If you think we can all squeeze in there."

I burst out laughing. "I think we can manage."

We piled into the car, and I found myself seated between Max and Tin, Monica and El opposite us.

"So where are you all from?" she asked, checking her phone.

"North," they chorused.

She paused, then slowly lifted her head to look at them each in turn before fixing her gaze on me, eyebrows raised. "OK," she mouthed, and I chuckled.

Monica could always make me laugh. Her sarcasm matched mine, even if she was more cynical at times and kind of hated Christmas.

"What's with the fancy ride?" I asked, hoping to take the focus off the elves.

"Alan organized it for all the senior management tonight. It's part of our bonus for hitting targets." Monica worked for a property development company that did work all over the world. She was the executive assistant to the CEO. I wasn't entirely sure what her job consisted of, but it paid highly enough that she could afford a two-bedroom in a good neighborhood without needing to get a roommate.

"What's with the matching coats?" She lifted El's hand by the sleeve, inspecting the beautiful fabric and golden fur trim. "These are really well made."

"What's with the bright green sequins?" he shot back, pulling his arm away.

She narrowed her eyes at him. I started to panic a little, my eyes flying between the two of them. Monica didn't take shit from anyone. I wouldn't put it past her to throw us out while the car was still moving.

But El smiled and lightened his rude tone. "It's Christmas Eve. I feel like outrageous outfits should get a pass."

A slow smirk pulled at El's lips, and Monica's breath hitched a little just as mine did the same. That wavy dark red hair, the freckles, the damn dimples when he smiled—coupled with the devious look in his eyes—were dangerous to women's underwear everywhere.

The car hit a bump just as it took a sharp corner a little too fast. With an "oof" I was knocked sideways into Max, Tin squishing me on the other side.

Max's arms wrapped around my waist to steady me as Tin righted himself.

With my nose pressed to the spot where the top few buttons of Max's coat were undone, I couldn't help but breathe him in—fresh snow and gingerbread. He reminded me of running out into the yard after the first snow to make a snowman, then drying off by the fire, gingerbread man in hand.

"You OK, Sadie?" His voice was low, his mouth close to my ear.

I pushed myself up and nodded. He held my gaze for a moment, and that glint I'd seen in Tin's eye lit up Max's, only it was red instead of white. I smiled, unable to resist the warm, fuzzy feeling that Christmas magic seemed to bring out in me—or maybe it was the attention of the gorgeous elf looking into my eyes and gripping my waist that was making me feel hot.

Slowly I pulled back, remembering there were other people in the car with us, and Max clasped his hands in his lap.

Monica and Elvis were both smirking at me. I cleared my throat and shifted in my seat.

Tin's hand landed on my knee, and I reflexively covered it with mine. He was looking out the window at the busy streets of the city center, completely distracted. Monica's eyebrows rose, and her smile widened.

Before anyone could say or do anything to make things even more awkward, the limo pulled to a stop.

I reached over Tin and pushed the door open before the driver even had a chance to come around, practically shoving the elf out onto the street.

We all piled out of the vehicle, and I took a few deep breaths of the cold night air.

"Thanks for the lift." I gave my friend a genuine smile.

"Anytime. This close enough? The mall is, like, two blocks that way." She pointed down the street.

"This is perfect." Max nodded as he took in the decorated street, huge garlands hanging over the traffic, and people hurrying down the sidewalk with bags of shopping.

Monica thanked the driver before he pulled away, then turned back to us. "It's still early. You have plenty of time before the stores close. You guys want to join the party for a bit? Technically it's for staff and family only, but you are my family, Sadie, and you three will fit right in." She pointed to the three elves.

"Oh, thanks, but—" I tried to rush through an excuse and get us moving, but El interrupted me.

"This is a Christmas-themed party?"

"Yep." She grinned.

"So, what're we talking? Decorations? Eggnog? Fruit mince pies?"

"We go all out. It's like Christmas on crack in there."

The three of them shared a look before Max shrugged. "Worth a shot. We're here already."

Monica gave me another amused WTF look. "Whatever that means. I'll take that as a yes. Come on, I'm freezing my tits off out here."

As they all moved to enter the building, I trailed behind, resigned to dodging questions from Monica but kind of happy to be going. Her company really knew how to throw a Christmas party. No expense was spared.

We crossed the cavernous lobby, and Monica swiped her card for the elevator, which took us to the twentieth floor. Her company occupied the top ten floors of one of the newer buildings in the city. The structure's modern, impressive architectural design allowed for a massive open area in the middle of the twentieth floor, with the higher floors curving around an actual indoor waterfall.

The elevator doors opened to reveal a party in full swing. The only thing rivaling the waterfall was the twenty-foot Christmas tree set up by the windows on the opposite side of the room. It was resplendent with white and gold decorations and glowing with hundreds of twinkle lights. The whole place was decked out in white and gold—garlands wrapped around all the railings, lights strung up everywhere, white poinsettias all over the place. There was even a snow machine tucked out of view near the top of the waterfall, sending soft flakes cascading down over the water.

El whistled low, clearly impressed. Max was nodding with a satisfied smile. Tin grinned and bounced on his toes, his eyes flying about the room to take it all in.

"I need to check on some things. Help yourselves to whatever you want." Monica waved in the general direction of a food table and walked off, removing her coat as she went.

Wait staff carried trays of food and champagne among the partying crowd, but the table was also laden with every Christmas food you could imagine. Tin made a beeline for it, stuffing an entire mince pie into his mouth and washing it down with eggnog even as he piled a plate high with frosted cookies, turkey slices, candy canes, and other things I couldn't make out.

Most of the people were in either Christmas sweaters or other holiday-themed outfits, at the very least, festive earrings or ties. Some were already dancing, "Last Christmas" by Wham blaring out of the speakers in front of a DJ wearing a Santa hat.

After spending hours in the freezing cold, my poor fingers and toes were finally thawing out in the warm building. It was actually *too* hot under my bulky coat, so I draped it over a chair in the corner.

I straightened my dress and turned to find three sets of elf eyes staring at me. Tin chewed slowly as his eyes trailed up and down my body. Max and El stood frozen in place.

"What?" I frowned and looked down at myself. The hem wasn't tucked into my tights or anything, and the Santa-inspired dress fit right in with what other people in the room were wearing. My family liked to dress up for Christmas too. Other than rushing to pile all the presents into my car, changing into the dress was the only thing I'd taken time to do before trying to leave the city.

It was red and long-sleeved, with a scooping neckline and white trim at the neck, wrists, and hem. The bottom flared out and ended around mid-thigh.

"Nice dress." El grinned, flashing me those dimples. Max nodded but averted his gaze. Tin bit into a cookie, his eyes still on my body.

"Uh ... thanks." I blushed and tucked a stray hair behind my ear.

Max smacked El lightly on the stomach and pointed to his pocket. "Anything?"

El pulled out the snow globe, and Max took it and held it up as we gathered around. It was looking more lively again—there was more detail in the trees and more light in the windows of the little cabin, in front of which had appeared a sleigh.

"OK. Good." Max nodded and pocketed it. "Let's get our Christmas on."

"Already on it!" Tin threw back the rest of his eggnog, and we all took something off his plate as he teasingly tried to lift it out of our reach. I managed to snag some shortbread and grabbed a glass of champagne from a passing waiter. The others all opted for eggnog.

Max and Tin wandered back to the food table and soon disappeared into the crowd, while I busied myself with checking out all the unique outfits—one guy was even dressed as a reindeer, complete with antlers and a fluffy tail.

El nursed his drink and leaned against the wall near the elevators, simply watching the festivities.

I said hello to a few of Monica's work friends I'd met before, making small talk for a while before working my way over to the tree. Craning my neck to see the top, I considered going up a few levels to get a better look at the star, but then I caught a glimpse of green velvet next to me and decided to stay put.

El put his hands in his pockets and followed my gaze up. The gold fur trim on his coat perfectly matched some of the ornaments.

"This tree is amazing." I smiled. Some of the massive baubles were almost the size of my head, with intricate decoration. I shuddered to think what they cost.

El leaned in to whisper in my ear, "You should see the ones at the Pole."

"Are you saying your trees are better than ours?" I flashed him a teasing smile.

He flashed me some dimple in return. "I mean, it's the North Pole. When it comes to Christmas, all our shit is better than yours. We're the OGs of Christmas."

I snorted, my shoulders shaking with silent laughter. After finishing the last sip of my champagne, I deposited the empty glass on a passing waiter's tray. The alcohol was making me feel warm and fuzzy. "I don't know that a tree's value has so much to do with how flashy it is or the size of the balls, you know?"

El laughed but nodded.

"My parents always get a real one—from a sustainable Christmas tree farm." I pointed at him to make sure he knew we weren't wasteful. "And most of the ornaments are really old and kind of worn, but they have sentimental value. I mean, I think one of my earliest memories is putting this particular red bauble with white snowflakes etched into it onto the tree. I remember how the lights shone through it and made it look iridescent. I thought it was magic." I chuckled. "Christmas trees always make me think of my family, you know?"

I tore my gaze away from the beautifully decorated tree to find El facing me, watching my face as intently as I'd been watching the tree. He had a melancholy look in his eyes, a sad smile that didn't bring out his dimples. My heart fell.

"Oh, I am such a jerk. I'm going on about family when ... I'm sorry. That was really inconsiderate of me." I chewed on my lip.

"So, Tin told you?" He ran a hand through his dark red locks. The sparkly lights made his hair look extra shiny.

"He told me his background, about how elves are recruited and all that, but he didn't share anything that wasn't his to tell."

El's smile widened, but it still didn't reach his eyes. They were dark green, just like Tin's. I couldn't stop noticing how similar they were in some ways and how different in others. How much of that was due to the Christmas magic?

"Tin was an orphan his whole life. I became one in my teens, so I do have some memories of family Christmases around a tree. It was a pretty small family, and the tree was nothing like this, but..." He trailed off.

I felt awful. "You really don't have to tell me anything. I'm sorry for bringing it up." I turned to face him fully and placed a hand on his arm, but he just kept staring at the tree, a faraway look in his eye.

"It's OK. I don't mind talking about it." He shrugged. "My mom was murdered by her asshole boyfriend when I was six. I never knew my dad. I don't think she knew who he was either. My nana raised me. We were all the other had. But she passed away when I was seventeen, peacefully, in her own bed. I was on the streets, sleeping in carboard boxes, when Shinny Upatree showed up in the middle of the night. I thought it was too good to be true at first, but eventually she convinced me I wasn't hallucinating." He chuckled, then turned to face me. "It's a pretty sad story, but I don't mind telling it, because I'm not alone anymore. I have those two dickheads." He inclined his head, and I turned to look. Max and Tin were in the middle of the dance floor, leading the festivities as "All I Want for Christmas" by Mariah Carey played.

I laughed and turned back to El. "I'm glad you have each other."

"Me too." He smiled, and his eyes flicked down to my lips. When he looked back up, there was that glint of gold magic in his eyes I was coming to expect anytime one of them looked at me intently.

A tree branch over his shoulder shook, making the baubles and tinsel bounce. My eyes widened as something shot out of the tree, trailing sparkly green magic behind it.

I patted El's shoulder and arm frantically, bugging my eyes out until he turned his head to look.

Whatever it was jetted up to the top of the tree, looped around it, then dive-bombed back down, disappearing into the branches and popping back out right next to our heads.

"Oh, hey there, little buddy." El grinned as a tiny green human *with wings* perched on the branch and waved maniacally at him. He extended his fist toward it, and the little creature gave him a fist bump.

El turned back to me and laughed. I was still wide-eyed, clutching the elf's velvet coat for dear life.

"It's just a Christmas faery," he explained. "Like the reindeer, it's attracted to us when we're in the real world. They're mischievous but harmless."

"What if someone sees it?" I looked around. Everyone was partying, and no one had even glanced in our direction.

"Relax." El grabbed my elbow. "No one can see them except us."

"Oh. OK." I released a sigh and relaxed my shoulders. "How come I can see it?"

He shrugged. "You're seeing all kinds of shit you're not meant to. Obviously, the Christmas magic has a plan here. Just roll with it."

"So, what do they do?" I leaned in to get a closer look, but the little faery startled and jumped back. Then it stuck its tongue out at me and flew off in a flurry of green sparkles.

El laughed. "They prefer crowds, parties, malls, that kind of thing. They just kind of flit about and do mildly annoying but amusing things. Swapping around the nametags on presents, refilling people's drinks so they get drunk, hiding all the scarves, and..." He trailed off as his gaze wandered up over our heads.

I looked up too. The little green troublemaker was floating above us, holding a mistletoe branch. It giggled, snapped its fingers, and flew off again, leaving the mistletoe floating in midair with its green magic.

THE MISTLETOE

El and I looked down at the same time. Suddenly, I was aware of how close he was standing, the texture of his coat under my palm, the heat of his hand cradling my elbow.

"It's tradition." He smirked and stepped even closer, his chest barely an inch from mine.

"Oh, well, we can't mess with Christmas tradition. It would ruin what we're trying to do here." I tried to keep my face blank, but my lips twitched into a smile as I raised onto my toes and closed the miniscule distance, pressing my breasts against his front and looping an arm around his neck.

He gripped my hip and brushed a stray hair off my forehead before cupping my cheek, all while our lips inched closer and closer until we were breathing each other's air. I was acutely aware of every hard plane of his chest against mine; the gentle, warm hand at my cheek; his pine-and-spice scent. It made me think of strolling through an evergreen forest while sipping mulled wine, with snow falling softly all around.

The chaos of the party around us disappeared as my lips finally met his. We kissed softly at first, our lips dancing sweetly. Then he dropped the hand from my face to wrap an arm around my shoulders and demanded more. I licked his lips, and he met my tongue with his, deepening the kiss in an intense, dizzying way that had me digging my fingers into the hair at the back of his neck, my other hand gripping the fabric of his coat.

A chorus of cheers and hoots went up, and I finally remembered we weren't actually alone. That faery may have been invisible to the rest of the room, but we weren't. With one last peck, we separated, and I buried my face in his neck—partly to hide in embarrassment and partly to drink in his intoxicating scent.

A pop song started to play and distracted the crowd once more, but when I raised my head, we still had the full attention of at least one person.

Monica stood right next to us, her arms crossed over her chest, a massive, slightly unhinged grin on her face.

"Whatcha doin'?" my best friend asked in that teasing voice I both loved and hated.

El frowned. "I thought it was pretty clear what we were—"

"No-no," she interrupted him. "Wasn't talking to you." She grabbed my arm and pulled me along behind her. "Come on, let's get a drink."

I threw El an apologetic look over my shoulder and mouthed, "Sorry." He smiled and waved me off.

Monica led me to the food table and grabbed a couple glasses of champagne. I realized I hadn't had dinner and was starving, so I collected a plateful of pastries and Christmas cookies and followed her to an alcove with some chairs.

As soon as we sat down, I immediately started stuffing my face to avoid saying anything. She watched me for a few moments, sipping champagne and doing her best impression of a Bond villain with narrowed eyes and a knowing smirk.

"OK, what gives?"

"Wha?" I spoke around a mouthful of croissant. "What do you mean?"

"What do I mean?" She threw her head back and laughed. "Well, you were just making out with the ginger, you were holding hands with the blond bubbly one in the car, and that was *after* you were making googly eyes at the black guy while falling all over his lap."

"There was a bump in the road. The car lurched."

"That's not really the point though, is it? What is going on with you and these guys?"

I groaned and took another sip of champagne to stall. "Honestly? I like all of them." I cringed, but Monica just grinned and clapped her hands.

"Excellent." She nodded. "I approve."

"Seriously? I feel like some kind of pervert. Why are you so excited about this?"

"Are you kidding? After the state that dickhead left you in, I haven't seen you this interested in anyone."

After my last boyfriend and I broke up, I went through a serious depressed state. I'd been on a few dates and had a one-night stand or two, but I just couldn't seem to connect with anyone. It had taken me a while not just to get over the relationship but to regain the self-esteem I'd lost by being with someone who constantly wanted me to change.

Monica had repeatedly offered me a job at her company, but it always came as reassurance that if I needed the job, I would have one. With Brian, it was always pressure to do something else, get out of retail, get a job that looked better. He dressed it up as wanting more for me, but really, he just hated introducing me to his lawyer friends as his girlfriend who worked in the lingerie department. It was about the way I reflected on him. He didn't actually care that I had goals, dreams I wanted to accomplish. Granted, those weren't exactly going anywhere at the moment, but at least I was working in an industry adjacent to the one I wanted to be in.

"So, what are you gonna do about it?" Monica asked.

"I don't know." I shrugged. "I know what I *want* to do about it"—we both giggled—"but I can't help feeling like maybe it's wrong on some level, that I'm being disrespectful by flirting with all of them at once."

"Bitch, please." Monica waved that away. "You just met these assholes. You're not in a relationship with any of them. You don't owe them jack shit. You're entitled to have a little fun. Are they being weird about it? Are they making you feel pressured or uncomfortable?"

"No, nothing like that."

"Are they being jealous or trying to compete in some pissing contest or whatever?"

"No. If anything, they seem amused when I show attention to one of the others. They've even, more or less, insinuated … that is to say, they kind of suggested that ... I think they might be willing to..."

"For the love of God, woman, spit it out!"

"All right! They've kind of hinted they'd be into sharing. Like, all at the same time kind of thing."

Monica watched me in silence for a moment, then burst into an excited squeal, clapping her hands and stomping her feet on the ground. "Oh my god! You have to do this!"

A couple of party people looked over at her shouting, and I shushed her. "Look, I'm not entirely opposed to it, OK? I just don't know if there will be an opportunity before they have to leave. I mean, we still have to get ... that part they need for their car."

"Make time." She leaned across the table, her eyes intense. "Do you have any idea how hard it is to get men into bed together? Sure, they're all up for a threesome when it's him and two chicks, but suggest throwing another dick into the mix and 'oh no, I couldn't possibly! I'm not gay!" We both rolled our eyes. "You have three, *three*, willing dicks. You have to do this for women everywhere. Also, so I can live vicariously through you."

"Can you not refer to them as dicks? They have names, Monica," I chastised her but couldn't keep a straight face, a full-bellied laugh escaping at the end.

She waved that off. "Where are they from again? That was kind of odd in the car when they all said 'North' at the same time. Like, upstate north? Or Canada north? Or the North Pole?" She laughed.

"Uh ... I'm not sure. They didn't really tell me much more." I washed the last of my croissant down with a gulp of champagne and got to my feet. "I have to pee."

I kind of did, but I mostly needed an excuse to avoid this line of questioning. I could never lie to Monica. We knew each other too well.

Thankfully, she didn't demand I sit back down and instead pointed up the massive staircase around the corner. "Use the one upstairs near my office. The one down here will be full with this many people."

"Thanks!"

I was up the stairs and down that corridor in a flash. After freshening up in the bathroom, I headed back out.

A gray-haired man in a suit appeared at the other end of the corridor, heading straight for me but staring intently at the ground, lost in thought. He was tall and skinny, but his suit was perfectly tailored, and he had a distinguished air about him. His cheerful Rudolph tie contrasted starkly with the worried look on his face.

"Alan?" I called out when we were just steps away from each other.

Monica's boss, the CEO of the company, looked up, startled.

"Oh, hello." He paused and gave me a small smile. "I'm sorry. I was so lost in thought I didn't even see you there. Sadie, right? Monica's friend?"

"Yes. Hi." I smiled back.

He glanced over his shoulder, looking sheepish. "I was so distracted I walked right past my own office."

I chuckled as we both started back the way he'd come. "What's got you so engrossed? Hope it's nothing too serious."

He sighed and opened his door, flicking the light on. "It's a work thing. I don't want to bother you. Go enjoy the party."

"There you are!" Max appeared in the doorway, grinning brightly, his unbuttoned coat revealing the tight T-shirt and perfectly fitting pants underneath. Why did they all have to have ridiculous bodies? It was distracting. "Thought we lost you."

"Here I am." I waved him over. "Max, this is Alan, Monica's friend. Alan, this is Max, my … friend."

"Friend" didn't feel right. I'd known him for only a few hours. Also, I was pretty sure what I wanted to do to him was more than *friendly*.

They shook hands and exchanged pleasantries.

"Now, what are you two doing up here?" Max asked. "Party's downstairs."

"You're right." Alan nodded. "You two should go down. Enjoy yourselves. I have to finish an unpleasant task."

"Work? On Christmas Eve?" Max propped his hands on his hips and tutted.

"Believe me, this is one thing I'd rather not do." Alan sank into his big leather chair and sighed.

"What's going on?" I prodded gently. "Sometimes it can help to talk about it to someone who's not involved."

He eyed us for a moment, then leaned his elbows on the desk. "All right, but there's only so much I can say—privacy and confidentiality reasons."

Max and I nodded and sat in the two chairs opposite.

"We've got a project—a big one. It's a large apartment building with retail space in a city that shall remain nameless. It's river frontage, and it's only recently been zoned for expansion. Anyway, we're in the late stages of acquiring the land. Most of the properties there are owner-occupied homes. We've made generous offers to all the residents, and most of them have vacated." He sighed heavily. "But there is one single mom in a two-bedroom holding things up a bit. She's accepted our offer but is having trouble finding another place— left it too late at this time of the year. Now, we work on a schedule with these things. They get warnings, dates by which they have to comply, and so on. It just so happens I have to issue an eviction notice to her. The paperwork is all drawn up. Everything's ready to go. I just have to make the call."

"Wait, this late on Christmas Eve?" I asked. I knew the corporate world never really stopped turning, but this was a little crazy.

"This is a cutthroat business. We have people who are paid very well to do these kinds of things, no matter what day it is. If I make this call, the notice will arrive tomorrow."

"On Christmas?" Max and I both sounded outraged.

Alan cringed. "It sounds callous, I know. But if you show any kind of weakness in this industry, it just invites trouble."

"Is it weakness? Or kindness?" Max asked mildly, no judgment in his voice.

Alan looked out into space, as if considering carefully.

"Alan?" I leaned forward. "What happens if you don't make the phone call?"

"Nothing." He shrugged. "Tonight anyway. The phone call will be made after Christmas, and she'll be evicted. She agreed to the offer— it's going to happen. It's only a matter of when. This isn't my job, really. I just didn't want the manager in charge of this project to have to throw a single mother and her three kids out of their home on Christmas."

"If you didn't want your manager to have to do it, then why are you doing it?" Max asked.

"Yeah." I nodded. "Clearly this doesn't sit well with you. You would've made the call already if it did. From the sound of it, no one will even notice if you wait a few days."

"You know what?" He leaned back in his chair, threading his fingers together and watching us with an amused smile on his face. "Fuck it. It can wait. Let the woman have a nice Christmas with her kids."

"Good for you." Max grinned at him, and I couldn't fight a smile either. Monica didn't talk about her work in any great detail, but I knew any property development company on that scale had to be involved in some harsh stuff from time to time. I'd just never heard about it firsthand.

"You know, I'd actually like to do more. Be better," Alan said after a while.

"How do you mean?" I asked.

"This business is tough. It's cutthroat and fast-paced, and we have to make hard deals all the time. I'm proud of what I've built here, but I do wish the culture of the industry were a little different. When I think about the kind of money we turn over quarterly and then about how many homeless people out there are struggling ... I just wish we could somehow do what our clients want but also do some good at the same time."

"Alan." I sat up. "If there's anyone who can find a way, it's you. I mean, look what you built here. You're the boss. All those people down there have to do what you say. And if you want to do something, then you're damn well going to do it."

"Where there's a will, there's a way." Max nodded.

Alan watched us with a contemplative look on his face, then leaned back in his chair. "Yeah. I am the damn boss. You know, I think I just got stuck in a rut. Between the company and raising a family, you just kind of fall into a routine, and you get busy, and shit seems too hard. I'm going to find a way to build multimillion-dollar projects for clients *and* provide cheap housing for the disadvantaged. Right after the holidays, we're implementing a charitable program."

He nodded and looked to the side, as if he was already planning out how it would work.

Max and I shared a satisfied smile. The snow globe in his pocket glowed, making us both look down, but we couldn't take it out and inspect it in front of Alan. Instead we just shared a secret fist bump under the table.

"All right! Back to the party, you two." Alan shooed us out. "I have a happy phone call to make, and then I'll join you."

We got up and walked to the door, and he called after us, "And thank you! Both of you. You were right, Sadie. Sometimes all it takes is a fresh perspective to get you thinking clearly."

"Anytime." I smiled and closed the door. Out in the hall, the boisterous sounds of the party below drifted up to us.

Max's fingers wrapped gently around mine. "You're amazing." There was that red glint of magic in his eyes again, taking my breath away.

I had to clear my throat before I could speak. "No, I'm not. I just talked to him. Sometimes, people just need someone to listen."

"You are." He stepped closer and leaned into me. "I can see why the Christmas magic sent you to help us. You have a pure heart."

I didn't know what to say. He was being so sweet. Also, he was hot, and I wanted to kiss his full lips. His fresh-snow-and-gingerbread smell was making me breathe him in like a creep, my eyes drooping closed as we leaned closer.

Our lips nearly touched, and then a loud laugh startled us.

Two drunk guys stumbled up the stairs.

"Max!" they chorused when they saw us, and rushed over.

"Bro, we've been looking all over for you." The slightly overweight one with reindeer ears laughed.

"Yeah, the costume competition is all set up, dude," his short buddy in a full bright red suit added. "We've been running this comp for years, but we never thought to do a prize."

They started to shuffle him toward the stairs. He looked over his shoulder at me longingly, but I shooed him away with a chuckle. A festive dress-up contest would help recharge the power core.

He nodded and turned to his new friends. "Actually, I had another idea. What if the prize was a donation to the winner's charity of choice?"

The two guys yelled and carried on about what a great idea that was all the way down the stairs. There was nothing like a party for making fast friends with total strangers. I had a feeling they'd be telling stories about the "elf dude" for years to come.

I started to wander after them, thinking I might try to find Tin and see if he wanted to dance with me.

As I passed one of the offices, the door swung open. A large hand wrapped around my wrist and a strong arm around my waist. Before I could even gasp in surprise, I was pulled into the dark room, and the door slammed shut.

THE JINGLE BELLS

As soon as the door slammed closed, I was shoved against the wall beside it. In the next instant, all six feet five inches of El's tall, muscular frame were pressed against me, and he was kissing me, wild and insistent.

I groaned into his mouth and kissed him back with just as much gusto.

He pulled away, breathing hard, and dragged his hands up and down my sides. "I want to tear this dress off you."

"You hate it that much?" I teased.

"No. I fucking love it. You're like every naughty Christmas fantasy come to life. But this fabric is just the wrapping. I want to see what's underneath." He hooked one finger on the neckline and dragged it down, exposing my cleavage.

"How about we compromise and peel it away carefully? I don't have anything else to change into."

His mumbled reply was muffled as he buried his face in my boobs. When he licked my cleavage, I gasped. He took his time, kissing and licking the tops of my breasts as his hands played with them over the fabric, pushing them up and kneading, his thumbs teasing the nipples.

But we didn't have time to take things slow. I wanted nothing more than to check into a hotel room and lock all three of them in with me for several days of debauchery, but we had a sleigh to fix, presents to deliver.

"That feels amazing," I breathed. "But don't we have to focus on the task ... the thing..."

"There's more than one way to spread cheer." He grinned against my cleavage and looked up.

I burst out laughing. "Oh my god. Do you all use the same lines?"

"Did Tin already crack that joke?" He chuckled but looked a little annoyed he'd been beaten to the one-liner.

I nodded.

"Son of a bitch." He shook his head.

"Are we gonna waste time talking?" I rolled my hips, rubbing up against the bulge in his pants. "It might land me on the naughty list, but I want to jingle your bells."

"Yes, ma'am!" he practically growled, then gripped my ass firmly and lifted me away from the wall. I wrapped my legs around his waist and my arms around his shoulders, grinning as he carried me across the room. I loved how strong and confident he was, how hard the straining muscles in his back felt under my touch. He was all man ...

er ... elf? Man-elf hybrid?

Anyway, he deposited me on the desk and kissed me again. His hands ran along my thighs and made me squirm against him, but his hips stayed just out of reach.

I made a frustrated noise and wrapped my arms around his waist, ready to drag him to me or climb him like a tree, but he laughed softly and pulled away.

He sat in the wheelie desk chair as I panted, both my hands gripping the edge of the desk.

His eyes drank me in slowly, from head to toe. Then he grabbed my left ankle, pulled the zip on my boot down with precision, and eased the shoe off my foot. It dropped to the carpet with a soft *thunk*. He repeated the deliberate movements with the other boot, then gripped both my ankles.

I was on the edge of my seat—literally—waiting to see what he would do next, ready and willing to follow his lead.

El's strong hands glided up my calves, around my knees, and up my thighs. The closer he got to the apex of my legs, the hotter and wetter I got for him. He teased me, running his thumbs over the sensitive creases, making me rock my hips to seek more friction.

But he kept going, his hands moving to my hips and up under the dress until he had the top of my tights in his grip. I lifted my hips, and he pulled the tights down, taking my panties with them.

He tugged the fabric down my legs, the tips of his fingers digging into my skin as he retraced his path.

When the tights reached my knees, he once again took my left ankle in his firm grip and pulled the fabric all the way off my foot.

After placing my foot on the chair beside him, he reached for the other ankle. Once the tights and underwear were completely gone, he put that foot on the chair too.

He looked me dead in the eyes, his lips parted, his muscular chest rising and falling. The golden magic glinted in his gaze as he gripped my knees and spread them, pushing the chair forward at the same time.

I gasped and gripped the table harder. With my feet propped up and my knees wide, I was completely exposed to him. All he had to do was lift the skirt.

He dragged his hands from my knees back to my hips, his grip less gentle this time, his touch on my inner thighs driving me wild.

I was holding back moans, and he hadn't even touched me between my legs yet.

And then he went from zero to a hundred in one second flat. He shoved the dress up, leaned down, and licked me in one smooth, confident stroke. I cried out and leaned back on my hands.

Elvis was so teasingly slow, then so intoxicatingly fast—I never had any idea what to expect. He curved his arms around my thighs to keep me steady and just went to town. He licked, sucked, and even used his teeth and had me racing head-on toward an orgasm within minutes.

I gripped the hair at the top of his head with one hand, threading my fingers into those soft auburn locks, keeping him exactly where he was as heat started to spread up my chest. I ground myself against his face as I chased the feeling, barely even trying to hold back my moans. Hopefully the party was too loud for anyone to hear anything anyway.

The click of a door handle made my eyes fly open, and the party noises briefly became louder before the door closed again. I whipped my head around, trying to pull away from El's relentless mouth.

Relief flooded me when I saw it was Tin and not an unsuspecting coworker of Monica's, because El wasn't stopping. His grip on my thighs tightened, his fingers digging into my flesh as he kept me in place and devoured me.

But I kept my gaze on Tin. His eyes immediately became hooded with lust. He took a deep breath, then let the air out through full, parted lips.

He sauntered around to the side of the desk to get a good look at what El was doing between my legs. Biting his bottom lip, he groaned and looked up at my face, and I couldn't hold it back any longer.

With a prolonged moan, I bucked against El's mouth, and my orgasm washed over me in hot waves.

El licked at me until I came down, then pulled away with a satisfied grin on his face.

"You guys know there are no locks on these doors, right?" Tin inclined his head to the door behind me.

El shrugged and stood. "Adds to the thrill."

"That it does." Tin nodded.

I was just trying to breathe while they talked.

"You look beautiful when you come." Tin brushed my flushed cheek with the back of his hand while El gently massaged the tops of my thighs.

I looked down, suddenly embarrassed for some reason by how openly they were talking about it.

"Would you like me to leave?" Tin asked. There was no judgment or expectation in his gaze. He just wanted to do whatever I felt comfortable with.

Apparently still incapable of speech, I bit my bottom lip and shook my head. I reached out to grip the back of his neck, pulling him in for a kiss. He kissed me as intently and gently as he had when I'd been up against that pine tree.

One of his hands was splayed on the table next to my hip for balance, but his other hand ghosted over my neck, his fingers tickling me as they trailed down. He grabbed one breast and massaged it, then the other, then kept moving down until he was cupping my swollen, wet lips.

I kept my eyes open the whole time, kissing Tin while I watched El.

El's eyes followed his friend's hand all the way down my body as he continued to massage my thighs. His coat was hanging off one side, revealing a toned shoulder, and the golden fur gleamed in the dim light.

Tin started moving his hand, rubbing me firmly, before sliding two fingers inside. I had to break the kiss to gasp, but Tin just redirected his focus to my neck and collarbone, licking and sucking, sending pleasure shooting straight to my nipples.

He gripped my bra strap and the collar of my dress with his teeth and dragged it over my shoulder. El was only half a second behind; the dress's wide scoop neck made it easy for him to pull down the other side with his hand until my breasts were spilling out.

They both pulled back to look.

"Perfect," El breathed as Tin nodded in agreement, his fingers sliding in and out of me slowly.

I couldn't take this torture any longer. I reached for El's pants, managing to pop the top button before he batted my hand away and finished the task himself. His pants fell around his ankles, and his cock sprang free. It was long and veiny, and perfectly straight. He stroked it slowly up and down as I reached for Tin's pants next.

Tin pulled away from me to undo them and push them down. He was a little shorter than El but thicker, the head engorged and just begging to be sucked.

"I want you in my mouth," I declared, finally finding my voice.

He moaned and looked up to the ceiling as if begging for control, then exchanged a heated look with El. I had no idea how many times they'd done this, how many women they'd shared, but in that moment I didn't care. I was just happy they were so comfortable with each other that they could both stand so close to me with their perfect, hard dicks out. I was just happy they were about to share *me*.

El held his hand out at his side, and golden magic sparkled at his fingertips as he brought his thumb and forefinger together. As the magic faded, a condom became visible—already out of the packet.

He slid it down his length as I watched, amused.

"You couldn't magic it directly onto your cock?" I teased.

He paused and canted his head. "Very good point. Next time."

"Say 'cock' again," Tin begged, his hand wrapped around his own hard length. "I love how it sounds coming out of your perfect mouth."

I turned to him and smiled. "Cock."

He groaned. "Naughty girl."

El lined himself up with my entrance, and we both looked down to watch as he slid into me. He pushed in slowly and with ease, letting us both revel in every single inch of connection until he was fully inside, his hips flush with mine, his hands gripping my waist. He held still for a moment and then kissed me. The sensations of him all around me—his hands on my body, his scent enveloping me, his hardness deep inside—were dizzying.

He broke the kiss and pushed me gently until I was lying flat on the desk. It was just wide enough for my body to spread across it, but my head hung off the other edge.

Tin moved around the desk. With my head tipped back, I was at the perfect height and the perfect angle for him. He stepped toward me, and as I took him into my mouth, his hips pushing forward, I applied a light suction. At the same time, El pulled out of me, and I moaned at the dual sensations.

They started slow, finding a rhythm—one thrusting forward while the other pulled back, or both thrusting into me at the same time—playing around with different timings until we found one that worked for all of us.

El started to slam into me faster and with more intensity, his big hands gripping my hips and spreading me open. Tin leaned over me and played with my breasts, kneading and rubbing and teasing the nipples, tugging and pinching as he pumped himself in and out of my mouth.

A small tree decked out in miniature baubles and bells sat on the corner of the desk, and as the two of them fucked me harder and faster, the decorations started to jingle with the movement. We'd joked about it several times, but we were now *literally* jingling the bells.

I tried to run my hands over the corded muscle in El's forearms, tried to reach over my head to grip Tin's ass, but the position they had me in was restrictive, and in the end, all I could do was splay my hands out on the desk and hold on for dear life. I surrendered completely to this moment, to the sensations coursing through my body, to the pure, exhilarating, intoxicating feeling of being consumed by them.

Tin was the first to come. His thrusts became jerky, his breathing shaky, and he stopped playing with my boobs and gripped the edge of the table.

Moaning, he spilled into the back of my throat as he doubled over. I swallowed him down—nearly choking on the sticky, warm cum pouring down my throat—and pressed my tongue against his length as he pulled out of my mouth. He slouched above me, his head hanging between his shoulders as he struggled to breathe.

El continued to pound into me—grunting, bells jingling, hands gripping. Tin dropped his weight onto his elbows and took one nipple into his mouth while he lightly pinched the other. It was enough to push me over the edge again, and I cried out as the orgasm crashed through me. My vision blurred as blood rushed to my head, my thighs trembling with wave after wave of pleasure coursing through my body.

El toppled over the edge only a few moments later, his moans matching mine, only deeper and more guttural. He buried himself deep inside me and ground his hips as he came.

After a few moments, El pulled out, and they both stepped away, all three of us breathing hard.

I let my body go completely limp as my breathing got back to normal, even though my neck was starting to hurt from hanging off the edge of the desk for so long.

As if he'd read my mind, Tin's hands cupped the back of my head and lifted it for me. He flashed me his cheeky grin, his messy blond hair falling over his forehead as he leaned down to give me a messy upside-down kiss that made me giggle against his lips.

He helped me push up into a sitting position. Halfway there, El grabbed my arms and pulled me the rest of the way up, then helped me pull my bra and dress back over my chest. He handed me some tissues from a box on the desk, planted a kiss on my forehead, and moved to pull his pants back up.

I cleaned myself up and reached down for my tights, but my knees buckled, and El grabbed me and lowered me into the chair, chuckling. He scooped up the tights and handed them to me, running his hand through his hair.

They were both buttoned up, T-shirts and coats straightened, once again looking perfect and good enough to eat. Meanwhile, I was still trembling, naked from the waist down, and having to sit because my legs wouldn't hold me up. It was hands down the best sex I'd ever had.

"Anyone else thirsty?" Tin scratched his belly. "I should get us some water."

"We'll go down together. Probably time to head off anyway." El leaned back against the desk and smiled at me. "If someone would just get her shit together and put her clothes back on."

I pointed at them both in turn and raised my eyebrows. "It's your fault I'm like this."

El grinned and held his right hand up, the back of it resting on his shoulder as if he were carrying a tray. Tin leaned forward and slapped it in a backward high five.

"Fuck yeah, it is." Tin nodded. They both looked very satisfied with themselves. I couldn't blame them; the feeling was warranted. We were, after all, completely satisfied.

I just shook my head and pulled on my tights and underwear.

I took my hair down and smoothed it before retying the ponytail. Tin appeared in front of me, twirling a sprig of mistletoe in his fingers that he'd pulled from a vase by the door. He tucked a stray hair behind my ear and gently slid the mistletoe into the top of my ponytail. I just about melted in the chair. He was so sweet and full of life.

El handed me my boots. Just as I was pulling up the zipper on the left one, the door burst open, and someone I'd never seen before rushed into the office. He was middle-aged and bald, kind of gangly. At the sight of three random people, he paused.

"Who are you?" The man frowned and looked around the dark space, taking in the mess on the desk. I was pretty sure this was his office, and I was pretty sure it smelled like sex.

I quickly finished zipping up my boot and sprang out of the chair, rushing around the desk.

"Hey, is this your office?" Tin sounded completely casual and relaxed even as we all rushed toward the door. "We just got a bit lost, man. Sorry."

The man crossed his arms over his chest and frowned. "Got lost, my ass. I know exactly what you three were doing in here, and you're going to pay to have my office cleaned professionally. Sanitized from top to bottom."

We hurried into the hall, the looks on all our faces something between guilt and barely restrained laughter.

"Hey, wait a minute, who the hell even are you people?" The man was starting to yell, coming out the door after us. "Do you even work here? How did you get in here? This party's for employees and family only. Hey, get back here!"

He was pissed off, and I could understand why. But we'd already started to flee, and the more he came after us and yelled, the faster we moved. We were like a bunch of teenagers caught out after curfew, and by the time we reached the stairs, we were running. We laughed as we sped down, but I'd be lying if I said there wasn't a bit of fear pushing me.

Max was in the middle of the dance floor, dancing with the same two dudes who'd dragged him off earlier and a whole bunch of other people none of us had ever met. I grabbed his arm as we passed, and the guys helped me push him into a run. He tried to ask what the hell was going on, but we all just yelled at him to run between peals of laughter, and he quickly got on board.

I took the lead, aiming for the stairs at the back of the corridor, but just as we approached, the elevator opened, and a couple of latecomers to the party stepped out. We rushed past them, and I jabbed at the Ground button, then the Close Door button repeatedly. Slowly, the elevator doors started to slide closed.

Our pursuer was still running toward us. He yelled and frantically pointed in our direction, but we couldn't hear what he was saying over the noise of the party. The doors shut before he could reach us.

As the elevator started to move down, I breathed a sigh of relief, and we all burst into laughter—bent over double, tears in the corners of our eyes, uncontrollable laughter.

THE SNOWMAN

About halfway down, we managed to get our laughter under control enough for Max to ask, "What the hell was that all about?"

That set the three of us off again, and he had to wait for the laughter to die down before he got an answer.

"We got caught with our pants down." El tried to keep a straight face, but a snort of laughter escaped. I could feel the giggles bubbling up again.

"Yeah, that guy chasing us caught us jingling some bells," Tin helpfully added, and I had to bite my lips to keep from laughing.

"Did you see the look on his face?" I couldn't hold it in any longer, and we all descended into another laughing fit.

Max crossed his arms. "You're telling me the three of you had sex in some poor guy's office and got caught?"

We all nodded, grinning and wiping tears from the corners of our eyes.

Max pinched the bridge of his nose, but we all saw his amused smile before he turned to face the opening elevator doors.

Still a bit worried the bald guy would send security after us, we rushed across the lobby and out into the street. It wasn't until we stepped outside that I realized I'd left my coat upstairs.

"Shit." I immediately started to shiver. The wind was icy. It would surely snow any moment now.

Tin rubbed my arms. "Where's your coat?"

"Forgot it in our rush to get away."

"Here." El shrugged his off and draped it over my shoulders, and I tucked my hands into the sleeves. The tips of my fingers barely reached the gold fur trim, but I was instantly warmer and surrounded by his pine-and-mulled-wine smell.

"Thank you. But won't you be cold? Maybe I can sneak back up and get mine."

"I'll be fine." He smiled. He was in nothing but black pants, a tight white T-shirt, and boots, but he looked completely unbothered by the cold. "Protection magic, remember?"

"Right!" I tucked the rich fabric closer around myself. They were so real, so genuine, that sometimes I forgot they were magical elves from the fucking North Pole.

"We probably don't have time for that anyway." Max held up the snow globe, studying it intently. "We got a good amount up there, but we need more."

The globe was now constantly emitting a faint glow, and the scene looked even more alive. The little trees even looked as though they were rustling in the breeze.

"Oh yeah!" Tin reached into his pockets and pulled out a handful of gingerbread cookies. He dropped them into the pouch Max pulled out.

"Nice. I got this." Max added reindeer ears attached to a headband, complete with bells.

El reached into the pocket of the coat I was now wearing and pulled something out in his fist. He held it over the pouch and opened his finger. What looked like green glitter sprinkled into the bag.

"Christmas faery dust?" Tin asked, and El nodded.

"That explains a lot." Max released a lighthearted sigh, then turned to me, putting the globe and pouch away. He reached over my shoulders and pulled El's hood up over my head. "Now, which way next?"

"This way." I pointed up the street. The main shopping precinct and mall were just around the corner.

Unlike the shady neighborhood I lived in, this part of the city was decked out in decorations and bustling with last-minute shoppers. The diners and restaurants we passed looked cozy and cheery, full of people cupping steaming drinks in their hands, and the shop fronts had elaborate displays.

The guys took it all in with smiles as we approached the main square. A Christmas market had been set up with stalls selling ornaments and hand-crafted gifts and vendors selling hot chocolate and roasted chestnuts.

"Ooh! Chestnuts!" Tin beelined for the vendor and ordered a serving as the others gravitated toward the temporary ice rink.

Most of the people with young children had gone home, but plenty of teenagers and couples were skating on the ice. A massive, twinkling tree loomed over the whole scene.

Tin returned with the roasted chestnuts, and we all huddled around him, devouring the treats in a matter of moments.

The chestnuts had helped warm my cold fingers. It was so chilly they probably didn't even need to use whatever machines kept the ice rink frozen. But there was still no snow. To the side of the ice rink, the grotto—potted, lit-up Christmas trees with open spaces and benches in between—was coated in soft powder from two snow machines. A group of young boys were pelting each other with snowballs, and I could just make out a snowman farther back, between the trees.

"Should we go for a skate?" Max suggested.

"No." I shook my head vigorously. I was painfully uncoordinated and had broken my arm the last time I'd attempted it in high school. "You guys go ahead, but I have no interest in strapping knives to my feet and repeatedly falling down onto a hard, cold surface."

They all laughed.

"We can teach you," Tin offered.

"You all know how to skate?"

"It's part of basic elf training." Max shrugged.

"Of course it is." I rolled my eyes. I thought I was a Christmas pro, but these guys were overachievers on a whole other level.

"Come on. It'll be fun." El nudged my shoulder. I bit my lip, remembering how painful and inconvenient it had been to have my arm in a cast for three months.

"The globe is loving this place." Max surreptitiously pulled back one side of his coat, exposing the snow globe poking out of an inside pocket. It was glowing in that way I'd come to understand meant it was charging.

I groaned. "Fine. But you better hope this 'can't get hurt on Christmas Eve' juju extends to me."

"Yes!" Tin punched the air and ran ahead to rent skates. I had no idea where they were getting money from—none of them had wallets that I could see. Hopefully they weren't just stealing things.

Within five minutes, I had the death traps strapped to my feet and was hobbling to the edge of the ice, gripping Max's arm for dear life.

Tin rushed ahead, El right on his heels, and started zooming around the rink, going forward, then backward, jumping and twisting like a pro. El just tucked his hands behind his back and bent down low, as if he were in a race. Without his coat, I could clearly see every toned muscle tensing and dancing under the fabric of his shirt as he moved languidly, gliding over the ice.

By the time I eased onto the ice on baby giraffe legs, the two of them had done at least three laps. I couldn't really watch them though. I needed all my focus to make sure I didn't face-plant.

"This was a bad idea," I muttered, every muscle in my body tense as Max slid around to stand directly in front of me. The others joined us, startling me as they skidded to a halt. I really wanted to whack them, but it was more important to hold on to Max.

Max held my hands firmly as Tin moved behind me and placed his hands at my waist. El stood shoulder to shoulder with me.

"Ready?" El asked, his hands still clasped behind his back. Annoying, smug, good-at-everything elf ...

"No." I frowned at my shaking knees.

"We got you, Sadie." Tin gave my waist a gentle squeeze.

"We won't let you fall." Max backed him up.

I nodded, and they all moved as one, Tin pushing me from the back, Max pulling and skating backward, and El keeping pace with us and giving me instructions.

"Bend your knees—it will lower your center of gravity and make it harder to fall."

I bent my knees.

"Lift your eyes. You don't need to look at your feet. You need to see where you're going."

I looked up, even though I could really only see Max's smiling face in front of me.

"OK, now push off with one foot while..."

El continued to give me instructions while the others held me tightly, guiding me gently along the ice.

Eventually I started to relax; my muscles loosened, and excitement slowly replaced fear. Tin let go first, zipping off to do another manic, complicated lap. Then, when I said I was ready, Max let go too. He kept skating backward, grinning at me as he got farther and farther away. Then he turned effortlessly and pushed into a faster pace.

I just moved one leg in front of the other steadily, reminding myself to bend my knees and look ahead.

"I'm doing it," I breathed with a smile.

"Yes, you are." El winked at me, then zoomed away too.

For a split second, I panicked without any of them nearby, but then I reminded myself I was managing just fine and continued to glide along at my glacial pace—pun intended.

They whizzed past me, calling things out and flicking my hair but never startling or shoving me so I would fall. I'd been deathly afraid of ice skating, but now I was actually enjoying it.

After a while, I started to get tired, and I realized I had no idea how to stop.

The next time a green velvet coat came flying past, I called out, "How do I stop?"

The coat had red trim—Max—and I turned my head to follow him with my eyes, but that meant I stopped looking where I was going.

I screamed and threw my arms out as the barrier rushed toward me.

My skates slammed into the hard barrier with a *thud*, but instead of getting thrown over the top, I was caught by a strong arm around my middle; another appeared just under my neck.

Max had one arm around my waist, the other propped against the barrier. Tin mirrored his position on my other side, his free arm thrown out to catch me across the chest.

Behind me, I could hear El laughing his ass off. I flipped him off over my shoulder and thanked the other two for saving my life.

"Anytime, beautiful." Tin kissed me on the cheek and skated off, chasing after El.

We'd come to a stop right next to the grotto with snow-machine powder. My heart was hammering, both from exhilaration and the fear of nearly dying an icy death. I heaved heavy breaths in and out, white-knuckling the barrier. Max just leaned on it casually next to me, rubbing my back and waiting.

"I'm good, I'm good, I'm cool," I said once my breathing was at a level that allowed me to talk.

"Good. You did great for someone who hasn't skated since high school."

"Thank you. I'm pretty proud of myself."

"You should be." He grinned—there was that red glint in his eye. His arm was still at my back, resting in the curve just above my ass, and his cheeks looked about as flushed as mine felt, not that it was anywhere near as obvious on his dark skin.

El flicked my ponytail as he zoomed past once more, and Tin whooped. I waved, and Max removed his arm from my back.

"Can't believe how good you guys are at this." I shook my head. "All Christmas things, really. I mean, I shouldn't be surprised, considering you're elves and all, but..."

"When you find something you really care about, it's hard not to throw yourself completely into it. Those two never had the picture-perfect Christmas, the amazingly decorated tree. Sure, they craved it, but they never knew what they were missing, not really. I had it, and I lost it." He paused, his unfocused eyes staring out at the fake snow falling over the potted trees.

The change in topic was a bit sudden, but I'd be lying if I said I didn't want to know more about Max. Although this didn't seem like a fluffy story. My heart constricted. I wasn't sure I wanted to hear it, but I'd listen if he wanted to share it with me.

"I had parents, a brother, and a sister. Both my grandparents died while I was in elementary school, but I had an uncle, a couple of aunts, cousins. I had a family, and we were close. We spent holidays together, taking turns to host. It wasn't perfect—no family ever is—but it was pretty damn good. I had people I loved to gather around the Christmas tree with."

He paused again, and the dread settling over me got a little heavier. I adjusted my stance, gliding the heavy skates on the slick ice to steady myself. The laughing and music faded as I watched Max's profile.

"Max." I placed my hand on his forearm and spoke gently. "What happened?" I didn't want to know. I *had* to know.

"It was summer. I can't remember why my parents had everyone over—someone's birthday maybe? I was seventeen and not paying too much attention to all that stuff. I was at that age when it's not really cool to hang out with your family. I didn't even wanna be there, spent most of the morning texting my friends. Anyway, there was a faulty gas line out back. It was such a nice day. They decided to do a barbecue. Everyone was in the backyard. I'd just walked out the front of the house to grab something from my car. My uncle lit the barbecue, and that was it. My whole family—twelve people—gone." He clenched his teeth and took a breath. "My mom and one of my cousins survived, but they both died in the hospital a few days later."

My mouth was hanging slightly open, my eyes wide with shock. It was the most horrific thing I'd ever heard. The thought of my family being ripped away from me—all those people at my parents' place, probably gathered around the fire by now, just gone—made me feel sick to my stomach.

"I had to organize funerals for twelve people. I was seventeen, for fuck's sake. I'd never even had a job. My mom had some distant family on the other side of the country, but I'd never even met them, and Mom hadn't spoken to them in over twenty years. They came to the funeral, but it was family friends who helped me deal with it all."

"I am so sorry that happened to you, Max. It's really awful. I can't even imagine ... god, I'm *so* sorry." I was rambling. I didn't know what to say.

He blinked and turned to look at me, as if he'd forgotten I was even there. "I've had a lot of time to deal with it. It'll never not hurt, but it does get easier to live with. Shit, I'm sorry for bringing the mood down." He gave me a weak smile and rubbed the back of his head, then lifted his hood, the red fur obstructing his downturned face. I reached up and yanked it right off again.

"Don't." I gave him a smile. "You don't need to hide from me. Or apologize for telling me something so personal. Thank you for sharing that with me."

"It's OK. Thanks for listening, Sadie." His smile was a little lighter that time, the look in his eyes a little more present.

"Anytime."

"You know, not a day goes by that I don't miss them, but I really am grateful to have El and Tin now. I don't know what I'd do without them."

"I think it's really great how close you all are."

"Yeah. And to think I almost said no when Shinny Upatree showed up and offered me a spot on the elf team."

"What? Why?" I was smiling, but my tone was incredulous.

He shrugged. "I was angry with the world. I went off the rails for a few years after it happened, blew all the insurance money, lost all my friends and anyone who ever cared about me. Last thing I wanted was to be reminded of what I don't have every Christmas. But Shinny was the first one to call me out on my bullshit. She told me I was throwing my life away and my family would be disappointed in me. I got so mad." He laughed. "Started throwing shit, yelling—at this three-foot-tall little woman. Then I realized she was right, and I went with her."

"And here you are."

"And here I am. With you."

His hand returned to my lower back as he angled his body toward me. He wasn't breaking eye contact, and neither was I—it didn't feel even remotely uncomfortable. We leaned in at the same time. I glanced down at his parted lips. His hand at my back inched around my waist. Our heads tilted, our lips barely a snowflake's width apart.

Someone screamed behind us.

We both startled and whipped our heads around to look.

The scream turned to hysterical laughter. There was a pile of teenaged girls on the ice just behind us, trying to get back to their feet through fits of giggles.

Their glee was infectious. I laughed and buried my face in Max's shoulder, taking a deep breath of his fresh-snow-and-gingerbread scent while I was there. His shoulders were shaking too, but his hand stayed at my waist.

Our moment may have been interrupted, but I had hope we would find another one before the night was out. I really liked Max—just as much as I liked Tin and El.

As I pulled away before our embrace could get awkward, I caught a glimpse of the snow globe peeking out of his pocket. "The globe likes this. Lots of Christmas cheer on the ice, I guess."

He glanced down. "Yeah, the globe likes this a lot. Almost as much as I like you."

"Oh." My breath hitched. I hadn't expected such an honest statement from Max. He seemed more reserved than his two mischievous friends. "I like you too, Max. Very much."

"Aww." A deep voice that somehow sounded like marshmallows had us both turning to look over the barrier.

The snowman I'd spied through the potted Christmas trees was suddenly right in front of us.

His body was a little lumpy, but the head was an almost perfectly round ball of packed snow. He had button eyes, a carrot nose, and a pebble grin. A red-and-green scarf was thrown around his neck, and more pebbles made up the buttons down his front. His stick arms were bent in front of him, as if he was pressing his hands over his heart.

If I hadn't already encountered a reindeer and a Christmas faery, I would've ended up on my ass on the ice when the snowman slowly turned his head to look between us, his pebble grin widening.

"You know, it's rude to eavesdrop," Max chided, but he sounded more teasing than actually upset.

"I can't resist a Christmas romance." That marshmallow voice was slow and deep.

"This is the strangest night of my life." I shook my head, my wide eyes on the animated pile of snow I was currently having a conversation with.

"Really?" He tipped his round head at me. "I've had stranger nights myself. This one Christmas in 1985, a certain lead singer of a rock band thought I was a giant pile of coke and tried to snort me."

It took him a while to get his story out in that slow, deep voice, but when he did, I burst into laughter. I leaned over the barrier and nearly lost my balance I was laughing so hard. Max had to steady me through his own giggles.

"Say," the snowman said once we got ourselves under control, "shouldn't you guys be, you know?" He pointed to the sky with a stick arm.

"Yeah. Our sleigh malfunctioned and crashed. Sadie here is helping us recharge and get back in the air," Max explained.

"I'd better leave you to it then." The snowman's body started to turn while his head remained in the same position. It was a little creepy and comical at the same time. "Hopefully this helps."

He waved a stick arm, and one of his pebble buttons floated away from his body as he slowly started to glide away.

Max caught the pebble and pocketed it.

"Was that Snowie?" Tin came to a stop next to us, and El slid in next to him.

"Yep!" Max nodded.

"Man, that guy's crazy." El shook his head.

Tin nodded. "He once told me there's this B-grade horror movie version of Frosty the Snowman that's loosely based on an acid trip the writer had in a snowstorm. Snowie saved his damn life but left him with one helluva vivid nightmare."

I had no idea what to say to that, so I just laughed some more.

"Come on, let's get moving." Max took my hand to lead me off the ice.

We returned the skates, and it felt good to have my booted feet back on solid ground.

"So, does last-minute shopping and gift giving fit the requirements?" I asked as we walked away from the ice rink.

Tin nodded. "Giving is a cornerstone of the Christmas spirit."

"OK, then let's head to the department store where I work. The decorations are stunning, and maybe I can replace some of the gifts that were stolen from my car." I just hoped I wouldn't bump into my boss.

As we headed up the busy street, we approached a skinny man in a terrible Santa costume, the beard hanging loose off his face, ringing a bell and collecting money for charity. The sign above his collection bucket read "Hearth Shelter."

I reached for my wallet, then realized I wasn't wearing my own coat. I sighed and flashed him an apologetic smile.

The man just winked at me. "Merry Christmas, pretty lady."

The guys all high-fived him as we passed, telling him he was doing a great job.

A little farther up the street, on a corner, I spotted a building with the same name—"Hearth Homeless Shelter and Charitable Organization" in simple letters above a door. The sign next to the door listed some of the services they provided—emergency housing, homelessness services, financial support, food bank, and several others.

I may not have had spare change to donate, but maybe I could do something better.

I pulled my phone out of my bra and dialed Monica. She picked up on the third ring, but I couldn't even get a word out before she yelled down the phone at me, "Bitch! You've got some explaining to do!"

THE GIFTS

I cringed, remembering the mess we'd left in that poor man's office and the fact that we'd just run off without telling her. "Hey, girl."

"Don't 'hey, girl' me, missy. What the hell did you do to Mr. Dover's office? He keeps demanding we call the police and make sure you pay to have it cleaned, but he won't tell anyone why." She laughed, and I knew I wasn't in any real trouble with her. "I had to get several eggnogs down his throat to get him to calm down."

"I'm sorry. And I'm sorry we left so quickly without saying goodbye. The guys are running out of time to get that part for their car, and Mr. Dover was chasing us, so…"

"Stop deflecting. What did you do?"

I glanced behind me—there was no one close enough to overhear. The three sexy elves were walking just ahead, giving me space.

I lowered my voice anyway. "We had sex."

"You dirty whore." By best friend was enjoying this too much. "Which one was it?"

"Two."

"Two what?"

"I slept with two of them. It was a threesome-type situation."

Silence. All I could hear on the other end of the line was the party in the background.

"Monica?"

"Yeah, I'm here. Sorry. I think I just had an auditory hallucination. I could've sworn I heard you say you had a threesome."

"Uh, yeah, I did."

"What?! Oh my god, Sadie! Which two? You come back here right now and tell me everything!"

I laughed. "I can't, but I promise I will another time."

"No. Now, woman!"

We were nearly at the department store entrance. The guys had slowed down to look at the elaborate moving displays in the windows as we passed.

"No. Later. I have to go. Monica, I need you to do something for me. A few things, actually."

She sighed dramatically. "What?"

"First, tell whoever needs to know that I'll make sure Mr. Dover's office is cleaned."

"Don't worry about that. I'm already taking care of it."

"Thank you. Second, I left my coat there. Can you grab it on your way out?"

"Sure, no problem."

"You're the best! And finally, I'm sending you a photo. Please make sure Alan gets it. I spoke with him earlier tonight—he'll know what it's about."

"You know, you're making a lot of demands for someone who's not giving me anything in return."

"You have my undying love. What more do you want, you greedy bitch?"

"Boo! You suck."

"Whatever. Eat a dick."

"Eat a *bag* of dicks."

"Whore."

"Skank."

"Love you."

"Love you too."

I hung up smiling and tucked my phone into the pocket of El's coat. When I looked up, all three of them were watching me with amused expressions.

"What?"

"You have a very odd relationship with your friend," Tin observed.

I shrugged. "It works for us."

"More importantly"—Max held up the snow globe—"what did you just do?"

The ornate globe was glowing brighter than I'd ever seen it. El and I both gestured for him to tuck it back into his pocket before anyone noticed.

"Remember how we were talking to Alan, Monica's boss, earlier at the party?"

Max nodded.

"Well, I had an idea about how he could do more good in the world—like he was saying. The Santa we passed was collecting money for a homelessness charity. I simply passed the info on to Monica so she could pass it on to him. I think it might be the kind of thing he wants to get involved in. We heading in?"

El shot forward and enveloped me in a hug, squeezing the air right out of my lungs. I wrapped my arms around his toned middle and breathed him in. His coat smelled divine, and I was constantly bringing it up to my nose for a hit of his pine-and-spice scent, but nothing beat getting it straight from the source.

"Thank you," he murmured into the top of my head, then planted a kiss there. When he pulled away, he was giving me a genuine smile that made his dimples pop out.

"What for?"

"That was a really thoughtful thing to do. As someone who spent time sleeping rough, charities like that are close to my heart. If Alan is serious about making a difference, this will change many people's lives."

"It was just a phone call." I chuckled. When he continued to look at me as if I were the sun *and* the moon, I leaned up and gave him a kiss on the cheek. "You're welcome. I hope it works out."

"Me too." He threaded his fingers through mine and took the lead into the department store.

Despite the fact that it was after ten, the store was packed. As someone who started to plan for Christmas while still sipping a pumpkin spice latte, it never ceased to amaze me how many people left gift shopping to the absolute last minute. Shoppers were browsing, some of them scrambling to get what they needed, and the registers all had long lines of customers waiting to be served.

Even with the somewhat hectic atmosphere, it was still one of the most beautifully decorated places in the city. The store spanned three floors of a historic building, and the owners had embraced the beautiful history and architecture instead of trying to modernize it too much. Of course, it had cameras and a security system and escalators, but it also still had its original carved staircases and tall wood-paneled ceilings, and the wreaths, garlands, lights, and baubles were draped over everything—not just the Christmas displays.

"Whoa," Tin breathed, his wide eyes taking it all in.

"You wanted decorations..." I gestured at the chaotic yet beautiful scene before us like a gameshow host.

"Right. So, what should we do?" El scratched the back of his head and stuffed his free hand in his pocket. He was so damn adorable.

"Shop, of course." I grinned. "What's Christmas without presents? And I do have all those stolen gifts to replace."

I sighed and thanked my lucky stars I had my phone set up to tap and go, although I internally cringed at the battering I was about to inflict on my credit card. I'd started my Christmas shopping in September and got as many gifts as possible on sale, and I'd been paying it all off for months. At least I knew exactly what I was getting for everyone. I just had to find everything and hope my credit limit was enough to cover it.

"Should we start at the top and work our way down?" Electronics was on the top floor, and I'd gotten my dad a new electric shaver with a fancy rotating head and a bazillion settings.

"Race you up the stairs!" Tin took off for the ornate staircase without waiting for a reply. El gave chase immediately, his slightly longer legs giving Tin's boundless energy a run for its money.

I shook my head and opted for the escalators, and Max followed close behind, still taking it all in.

El and Tin were playing around and laughing when we made it upstairs. Neither was particularly winded from running up three flights.

I made a beeline for the small appliances section and scanned the shelves until I spotted the model I'd originally purchased two months ago during a half-off sale. It was now full price, and I cringed but took it off the shelf anyway.

We wandered past the different displays, rows of mattresses, and shelves of more gadgets than any of us knew existed.

"Egg maker?" Tin held up an appliance about the size of a toaster but shaped like an egg with the bottom cut off. He lifted the lid to reveal slots for six eggs. "Surely this technology peaked with the whole 'pot of boiling water' system."

"I see your egg maker"—Max leaned around the display next to us and held up a round white thing—"and raise you an automated floss dispenser."

"*No*. Really?" I laughed as Tin groaned, and we both leaned in to make sure he wasn't trying to trick us. "Why?"

"Right?" Max returned it to the shelf.

"I mean, it wouldn't even save you any time," Tin pointed out. "If anything, it'll cost you money because you'll constantly be replacing the batteries. Who buys this crap?"

"The same people who think weirdly shaped vibrating things make an actual difference to back problems?" El popped his head over the shelf next to us and leaned on the top, holding up that "wand"-shaped massager most people knew about.

We all burst into laughter.

"I think we all know that no one uses that particular model to get knots out of their neck," I said.

"Oh?" El put on his best impression of an innocent look. It was kind of ruined by the amused smirk. "Whatever are they used for, Sadie?"

I flipped him off. "You know very well what they're used for, Elvis."

"Care to demonstrate?"

"With that thing? No thanks. My *actual* vibrator, which was *actually* designed for female pleasure, is way better, thank you very much."

"Say 'female pleasure' again," Tin growled into my ear, his hands going to my hips as he pressed against my back.

"Oh! Hey, look! Televisions." Max didn't wait for a response before rushing down the aisle.

I extracted myself from Tin's hold, and we moved to follow Max.

As I passed the shelf where El had been standing just a moment earlier, I spotted a woman. She had curly black hair and looked like she was in her thirties, and she was holding the same wand in her hand, a slight frown on her face. She looked at me, then down at the wand, then at me again.

I leaned in and whispered the name of a website that sold good-quality, safe toys and winked. "Their packaging is discreet."

I rushed to catch up with the guys.

They were standing in the middle of the TV section, surrounded by dozens of different-sized screens all playing the same movie—*The Grinch*.

I wedged myself between El and Max. El draped an arm over my shoulders, but Max didn't move away, leaving his arm pressed against mine.

"This is my favorite movie," Tin announced, his eyes glued to the screens.

"They're all your favorite," Max murmured.

It was nearly at the end; the Grinch was at the top of the mountain as the Whos began to sing. The four of us got engrossed in the tail end of the story, watching as the Grinch's heart grew three sizes and he returned all the presents.

"I suddenly feel like roast beast," Tin said as the credits rolled.

Max rolled his eyes. "You stuffed yourself at that party. How can you still be hungry?"

"I burned it all off." He wiggled his eyebrows at me.

I would've laughed and cracked a joke too, but over Tin's shoulder, I saw my manager marching down the aisle, coming straight for us. The fluorescent lights glinted off his shiny bald head.

I gasped. I could not deal with him spotting me. We'd waste the rest of the night having to listen to him berate me for leaving work early and not going to see my family like I said I would, and we'd never make it back to the sleigh in time.

I flipped the hood of El's coat up and hunched into his embrace, tucking my hands between us and resting my forehead on his chest.

"Uh ... Sa—"

"Shh!" I cut Max off before he could say my name, then whispered to El. "Tell me when the bald guy is gone."

He nodded against my head and rocked me from side to side for a few moments.

"He's gone," he said before dropping his arms from around me. I kept my face plastered to his front—partly because he smelled amazing and partly because I couldn't be sure.

Slowly, I pulled the hood back and looked around El's broad frame to check that the coast was clear. My manager, Ed, was nowhere in sight. I breathed a sigh of relief.

"What was that about?" Tin asked.

"That was my boss. If I get caught in here, it's not gonna be pretty, so if you see him coming, let me know."

"Hey there!" A bright voice made us all turn around. "Can I help you folks with the TVs?"

A young guy wearing the uniform I wore to work every day was smiling brightly at us. It was a big store, and I didn't know everyone, but his nametag said "Mark."

"No thanks, Mark." Tin slapped him on the back. "We were just watching *The Grinch*."

"Oh. Haha!" Mark laughed awkwardly. "Yeah, that's a great movie."

We walked away, in search of the rest of the presents I had to replace.

As we worked our way down through each section, I gathered a robe and slippers for Mom, a necklace for my sister, and vases and T-shirts and ties and toys for cousins, nieces, and nephews.

In the menswear section, Ed's bald head once again appeared a few rows over, and I pulled Max down into a crouch with me behind a rack of leather coats.

"Why am I hiding?" Max asked. "He doesn't know *me*."

"Shh." I just covered his mouth and waited until Ed moved off. Then I wondered if I should get my dad cufflinks to add to his present—even though all the gifts I'd gathered so far would cost me more than I'd originally paid for them.

In the accessories department, right between ladieswear and intimates, Ed strode up to lean on the counter and chat with the workers there. They looked completely frazzled, rushing around to replenish displays between serving customers, but he just leaned ... Casually ... *Asshole*.

I pulled my hood up and acted very interested in a spinning display of earrings while Tin did his best to make me laugh. He held up pair after pair, each one bigger and more ostentatious than the last, and checked himself out in the mirror.

When I thought I might explode from trying to hold in the giggles, I walked away, grabbing the first purple thing I saw. Cousin Annie had a thing for purple; I figured it didn't really matter that they were three times the size of anything the petite woman wore or that they cost four times what I'd planned to spend on her. Although she had gotten me a very expensive-looking handbag for my last birthday, so maybe I should be spending even more?

"Hey, Sadie, is any of your stuff here?" El asked. I'd been so busy obsessing over gifts and keeping an eye out for Ed, I hadn't realized we'd walked into the lingerie section.

"Oh! No. My stuff isn't in any stores." I laughed and ducked my head.

"How come?" He frowned.

"I don't know. I'm a nobody. I occasionally sell a few sets online, but working full time, I hardly have time to design and make new pieces, let alone work on marketing and getting my stuff seen." I shrugged.

"Can we see?" Max asked.

"Yeah, show us." Tin grinned.

"You want to see my underwear?" I asked teasingly.

"Yes!" Tin nodded.

"No." Max's eyes widened. "I mean..."

"We want to see your work, Sadie." El crossed his arms and fixed me with a serious look.

"Not right now," I said. "We have too much to do. We should move away from here. This is the section where I usually work, so I'm bound to bump into someone I know."

They let me rush past, my arms full of gifts. I'd even handed a bunch of things to each of my elf helpers. They followed me silently to the ground floor, but I heard them whispering on the escalator behind me.

When we reached the bottom, I turned on them. "What?"

They all snapped their heads up to look at me, eyes wide. The snow globe was poking out of Max's pocket, and he tucked it back inside.

"It's stopped charging. It was doing all right, but it seems to have stalled for some reason," Max explained.

"Oh." I shuffled my feet. There I was getting worked up and being shitty to them because I thought they were whispering about me behind my back, when in reality, they were just worried about thousands of children getting their gifts on Christmas Eve.

"Sadie?"

My spine stiffened at that voice, and the "sorry" I'd been about to say turned to ash in my mouth.

I prayed that I'd heard wrong, that there was another Sadie nearby, that it wasn't him. But then he tapped my shoulder, and I turned to come face to face with my ex.

THE CHEER

Brian had blond hair, but it wasn't soft and shiny like Tin's—it was kind of wiry and dull—and his brown eyes were swimming with amusement. He tucked his hands into the pockets of his wool peacoat, which he had on over an expensive suit—he always wore an expensive suit. Even when we were together and I was into him, for some reason, I'd never gotten to tear the suave outfits off him. He always insisted on undressing and neatly draping the expensive fabric over a chair before we had sex. What the hell did I ever see in this douche?

"I thought it was you." He smiled, as if he hadn't "popped in" to the store and "bumped into me" at least once a week since we broke up. "I was hoping to bump into you."

"Hey, Brian." I sighed and shifted all the stuff in my arms. "Actually,

I'm—"

"Did they change the uniforms or something?" he interrupted. He pointed to the guys coats behind me, then gestured up and down my body at El's matching coat. "Christmas all the way?"

"No, they didn't. I'm actually not working tonight."

"Oh? Then what are you doing here? And what's with the matching outfits?" He frowned at the guys again, looking them up and down in that way men do when sizing each other up.

I decided not to get into it. I just wanted to be as far away from him as possible. "Look, I really need to get moving and—"

"Yeah, yeah, I'm in a hurry too," he interrupted me again. "Listen, I just need your help real quick. Can you tell me which bra and panties are a good brand or whatever?" He rolled his eyes with a smile.

"Excuse me?"

"Like, what's a good one? Nice lingerie." He leaned over with his hand next to his mouth, as if he were telling me a secret. "I left Tania's gift to the last second."

Tania was the woman he was currently seeing. He'd mentioned her the last three times we'd "bumped into each other" ... at my work ... while I was *working*.

"You want me to help you pick out panties for your girlfriend?" I raised my eyebrows.

He just shrugged as if it was no big deal. "Yeah. I mean, you know your shit, right? This is your thing."

"You didn't seem to think I 'knew my shit' when we were dating," I half mumbled, unable to keep the comment in.

"What? I thought we were cool, Sadie."

"Wait a minute." El handed the few gifts he was carrying to Tin and stepped forward. "You're asking your ex to help you pick out lingerie for your current girlfriend? Dude..." He just shook his head.

"What?" Brian frowned. "What's the big deal? Who are you?"

"Bro, that's pretty disrespectful to both women." Tin stepped forward, then deftly caught a box of perfume that slipped off the pile of my shit he was holding.

"And who are *you*? And who's that guy?" Brian pointed to Max, who was standing back but frowning at the whole exchange.

"You know what?" El pointed a finger at Brian's chest. "I'm Sadie's—"

"Stop!" I cut him off. "Brian, it's none of your business who they are. We broke up six months ago—*nothing* I do is any of your business anymore. And it's weird and inappropriate to ask me to help you buy lingerie for your girlfriend. And stop coming here, for fuck's sake. Find somewhere else to shop. Now, we're leaving."

I turned and started walking away. My new elf friends followed with proud, smug looks on their faces.

"What the fuck, Sadie?" Brian called after me, sounding bewildered. "I thought we were cool? Why are you being a bitch?"

I whirled around, my blood boiling and my hands shaking. I'd kept it all in—reluctant to cause more drama by saying anything to him, ranting to Monica instead—but now it came bursting out of me.

"We are not *cool*, asshole! You treated me like shit, and you're still doing it! Leave me the fuck alone!"

"*Don't* call her a bitch." Max's voice was low, his face completely devoid of emotion, yet the words came off more menacing than if he'd gotten in Brian's face and screamed them. Brian's eyes widened, and he took a small step back.

Several people had stopped to stare at my outburst. To make matters worse, I spotted my boss hurrying toward us through the crowd.

"Shit," I muttered, and we rushed away, getting lost in the shoppers and weaving through displays.

The toy section was the messiest area of the store—it had been practically torn apart by people desperate to make sure their kids had the shiniest new things for Christmas. But the chaos made it easy to hide in a back corner.

"Sadie, you OK?" Tin asked, his usually chipper voice low. They all watched me with worried faces.

"Yes." I gave them a weak smile. "No. I don't know. He gets to me, you know? And the worst thing is, I just realized I've been *letting* him get to me. *Ugh!* And I still don't have all the gifts I need and..." I trailed off, my mouth opening and closing like a fish.

"I'm really glad you stood up for yourself, loud as it was." El gave me a wry smile.

"Uh, guys." Max held up the snow globe. "We have bigger issues."

We all leaned in to look. It wasn't as dull and lifeless as it had been at the very start, but it had certainly lost some of the magic that had appeared at the ice rink and the homeless shelter.

Tin took it and brought it up close to his face, his brow furrowed.

"Oh no," I breathed. "What happened?"

They exchanged loaded looks, then Max sighed and explained.

"It seems the power core is more connected to you than we thought, Sadie."

"Me? What? How?"

He rubbed the back of his neck. "We're not sure."

"We suspected it was related to your ... enthusiasm for the holiday spirit to an extent," El added, "but it seems you have more effect on it than we thought."

"I don't understand."

"We don't fully understand it either." He shrugged. "Like we explained earlier, we don't know all there is to know about Christmas magic and never will. But it did malfunction just as we were passing over you. What were you doing just before we crashed?"

I cleared my throat and looked around awkwardly. "I was grumbling about passive-aggressive texts from my family and how this was the worst Christmas ever. I'd just decided to go back up to my apartment, tear down all my decorations, get trashed, and watch a horror movie."

Tin looked horrified as he tucked the globe into his pocket, slightly angling his body away as if to protect it from me.

Max pinched the bridge of his nose.

El just smirked. "Look, I'm not saying your giving up on Christmas was what made us crash, but it probably contributed to it. And all the stuff we've been doing, it's definitely helping to recharge the power core, but it seems to get the biggest boost when you do something particularly ... nice."

"Like the kids at the concert," Tin reminded me.

"And convincing Alan to get involved with the homeless shelter," Max added.

"And now you're *not* feeling particularly cheerful and..." El cringed and gestured to Tin's pocket.

My heart sank.

I'd literally ruined Christmas. I was like the Grinch but worse.

Tears welled in my eyes. Every time I saw Brian, he managed to make me feel like shit. Now, on top of all that—on top of the stolen presents and derailed Christmas Eve—I was supposed to be responsible for fixing everything?

I looked between them with wide eyes, clutching the clothes and boxes and other gifts closer to my chest. "I can't do this. It's too much pressure. I'm just … nobody."

A tear escaped and trailed down my cheek as my breathing got shallow.

They all frowned, but it was Max who stepped forward. "You are *not* nobody."

I just shook my head and lowered my gaze to the ground. That tequila and slasher flick were sounding pretty good again.

Max handed the items he was holding to El, then took half of mine and shoved those on top.

"What are you doing?" I sniffled as he took the rest of my presents and loaded them onto Tin's pile.

"Just give us a minute, guys." Max grabbed my hand and pulled me down the aisle.

He dragged me to the edge of the toy section, where an elaborately decorated "Photos with Santa" area was closed off and dark. The pretend Santa had gone home hours ago—there were no more kids around to take photos.

Like the rebel I didn't think he was, Max lifted the red velvet rope blocking off the entry and pulled me through the archway, which was resplendent with garlands, dripping with bows and candy canes.

"I don't think we're supposed to be here," I murmured.

He just shrugged. "I'm an elf. We practically run this shit."

Despite the dreadful mood I was in, I cracked a smile.

Once we were around the corner, out of sight of the bright store beyond and off to the side of the big red chair, he finally stopped and turned to me.

With a sigh, he propped his hands on his hips.

"I'm sorry." I rubbed my arm. "I don't think I'm cut out for this."

"Bullshit." The word was forceful but not angry or frustrated. I didn't feel like he was upset with me, but the assertive tone coming from the usually quiet, reserved Max was surprising. "Sadie, you were made for this."

When I didn't respond, he kept speaking. "You rushed to see if we were OK when we crashed without having any idea who we were. *You're caring.* You've listened to all our sob stories and not for a second made us feel any less normal compared to your full, happy family. *You're kind.*" He started to tick things off on his fingers. "You've seen as many Christmas movies as Tin. You dress up and decorate without being forced to. Your eyes light up with wonder at every new Christmas-magic element we show you. You make a genuine effort to not only get thoughtful gifts but spend time with your family at Christmas. Despite the slight bump in the road when everything seemed to go wrong at once, you fucking love Christmas. From everything you've told me, you always have.

"I don't know why that damn globe is so connected to you"—he waved his hand dismissively—"and we probably never will, but if you think for one second that you can't help us recharge it, you are so damn wrong."

"You make some very good points," I grumbled. His sweet speech had made a warm, fuzzy feeling appear in my chest. I so badly wanted to get over my insecurities and just get back to work, but they were hard to let go of. "I just … I don't know. It's a lot of pressure, and I kind of feel like I'm holding you back."

Max grabbed both my hands and guided me over to a bench off to the side. During the day, it was lined with kids waiting for their turn with Santa; now, it was just Max, facing me, his legs on either side of the seat.

"I don't know what that asshole did to you, but I promise, every negative thing he ever told you about yourself was a lie. You can do this. Christmas is kind of my thing, and I can see the spark in your eye." As if on cue, the red glint of magic glowed in his gaze, mesmerizing me and making me smile. "Please, Sadie, we can't do this without you."

I stared sidelong at his earnest face and thought about what he was saying—*really* thought about it. Maybe he was right. I'd gotten wrapped up in my own shit, and I'd let Brian get under my skin again instead of thinking of the bigger picture.

Taking a deep breath, I turned to face Max fully. "OK, you're right. I can do this. *We* can do this. I'm sorry I got so sidetracked and overwhelmed."

He gave me a brilliant smile and squeezed my hands. "There she is."

"Shit!" Now that my crisis was over, panic hit me. "What time is it? Are we gonna make it?"

"Calm down." Max's firm grip on my hands kept me from shooting up off the bench. "We still have an hour or so, and despite it dulling a bit, the globe doesn't have that much charge left to replenish. With you back on board, we got this."

"You sure?" The kids, the presents!

"I'm sure. Now, come here and hug it out." He dropped my hands to open his arms out wide.

Without hesitation, I leaned forward and wrapped my arms around his neck, my fingers gliding through the soft red fur on his coat.

His fresh-snow-and-gingerbread smell assaulted my senses in the most wonderful way. I wanted to take a deep breath—the kind of breath you take when you open the door and realize it snowed all night. I also wanted to lick him, the way I lick the icing off gingerbread cookies.

I pulled back slowly, but his arms tightened before releasing me— he wanted to let me go about as much as I wanted to back away. My cheek scraped his. He turned his head just a fraction in my direction, his eyes downcast. My breath hitched. And then we were kissing.

It was tentative at first, his lips soft and gentle against mine. Then it built. I don't know if it was me or him who pushed it further, but all of a sudden, his tongue was in my mouth, and mine was pushing right back.

He stroked my cheek with his thumb, his other hand sliding up my ribs. I scooted forward on the bench until I was in his lap, my legs draped over his on either side of his hips.

He was straddling the bench, and I was straddling him as we kissed passionately, our lips not parting even for breath.

With a confident hand at my upper back, he pressed me against his chest. I gripped his shoulder tightly and rolled my hips, finding him already rock hard for me. He groaned, which only spurred on my own arousal.

He was so hard it was almost painful as I ground against him. Pleasure built, heat spreading through my body.

I moaned into his mouth, and he gripped my hips.

He finally broke the kiss to press his forehead against mine, his hot breath washing over my face. He stared down, watching us writhe against each other as his hands guided my movements.

"Shit." He groaned, then gripped my hips tighter and stilled beneath me.

We both breathed hard for a moment as the sounds of a bustling department store slowly trickled back in.

"We don't have time for this." I leaned away, looking up to the ceiling to catch my breath, even as my body protested, *demanded* I keep going, roll my hips just one more time. My core was pulsing with need.

"We don't have time for all the things I want to do to you," Max ground out, his voice gravelly and intense.

I looked back into his eyes, a little surprised and even more turned on. "It's always the quiet ones," I teased.

He chuckled and shook his head. Then he smacked my ass, the movement lightning fast and right on the line between playful and stinging.

I jumped and made a startled sound.

He stood with me in his arms and stepped over the bench before lowering me to the ground, letting my body slide down every inch of his hard one.

"To be continued," he declared and stepped back to adjust his prominent erection.

I gathered myself as best I could, tightening my ponytail and smoothing my red dress, then followed him back out into the store.

It was lucky the green velvet of his coat fell to just above his knees, preventing me from staring at his ass, because that was all I wanted to do in that moment. The coat, however, did nothing to hide his broad, defined shoulders—the same ones I'd just been clutching as I …

"Where'd they get to?" He turned to me and propped his hands on his hips, making me drag my mind back out of the gutter.

"Hmm? What?"

Max chuckled. "Head in the game, Sadie. Can you see El and Tin anywhere?"

"Oh, right! Uh…" I looked around, not spotting them, but then the distinctive sound of Tin's infectious, happy laugh came from near the middle of the store. I pointed in that direction, a triumphant look on my face. "See! Head totally in the game. I'm helping already."

Max just gave me a skeptical, if amused, smile and followed me.

We found El and Tin at the gift-wrapping station, right between the elaborate Christmas tree and the layaway and service counter. They had the attendants—a busty woman and a short guy with amazing chestnut hair, both in their twenties—roaring with laughter. All four of them were draped in ribbons as Tin expertly wrapped a very large box with sparkling red paper.

El was standing off to the side a little, also wrapping something. Not that he was going unnoticed—the attendants were checking them both out and flirting unashamedly, batting their eyes and touching them at every conceivable opportunity.

"Sadie!" Tin called out as we approached, putting a flourish on the white ribbon he'd just tied.

"Hey, you." I smiled at him, and he had eyes only for me. Not that I was jealous—we'd only just met, decided to save Christmas together, and had a bit of a threesome. No biggie. Not like I owned either one of them. But it was nice to see I had his full attention.

"You back?" El raised an eyebrow.

"I'm back, baby." I nodded.

He held his fist out for a bump, and I obliged.

The two attendants smiled at us politely, but their raucous laughter had died down significantly.

"We've been making some great progress here." Tin gave us a meaningful look and glanced down at his pocket. The top of the globe was only just poking out, but I could see it glowing faintly.

I breathed a sigh of relief. I hadn't realized it, but I'd been worried my antics had thrown us completely off schedule.

"Yes." The female attendant beamed as another customer walked up to the service desk. "With El and Tin's help, we've smashed through all the donation gifts. Only got a handful to go."

"Oh, that's great." I smiled. The store ran a program where shoppers could purchase items to donate as gifts to families in need. They were all wrapped up by staff and delivered on Christmas Day by volunteers. But I was distracted by the conversation on the other side of the service counter.

The woman who'd just walked up was in a puffy coat similar to mine, her hair in a messy bun. With hunched shoulders and bags under her eyes, she looked about as done with Christmas as I'd been when three actual elves crashed at my feet.

"Is there nothing we can do?" she pleaded with the chestnut-haired attendant. The man looked sympathetic but shook his head, saying something I couldn't hear.

"OK, let me just call my husband." The woman turned away and pulled out her cell phone.

"We're wrapping all your presents too, Sadie." Tin drew my attention back, but I kept one ear on the woman.

"The gifts you were getting for your family," El explained. "We thought we'd save you some time and wrap them. We've done two but should have the rest sorted pretty quickly."

"Uh-huh. Wait, just..." I waved them off, my full attention on the woman.

"I know, Mike, but they won't do anything ... Forty-five dollars short ... You try telling my asshole boss that. I'm sure the shortfall will be sorted out in next week's paycheck, but that doesn't help me now ... Yeah, he really is ... I'm gonna look for a new job after the new year ... Yeah ... That doesn't really solve our current problem though ... Mike, how are we supposed to explain to a six- and eight-year-old that they can't have their Christmas presents until after the new year?" She threw her hand up and let it flop to her side.

I turned back to the guys. They were all watching me listen in unashamedly to a stranger's private conversation.

"Stop wrapping those," I ordered. El immediately lifted his hands, palms out, and stepped away from the table. "I'm not getting any of them."

Now they all looked confused, but everything was suddenly crystal clear to me. I didn't need to break my bank buying all that stuff. My family wanted me home for Christmas. Not the presents, *me*—their daughter, sister, cousin, niece, granddaughter. They'd understand I'd been robbed.

And losing track of that was exactly what had made the globe fade. I'd gotten fixated on buying things when the point was to be giving—in spirit and action, not in material things.

"I'd like to purchase the few items the guys have already wrapped and donate them, but I'll leave the rest," I told the guy at the service counter without preamble. "I'm so sorry for the trouble. Can you please ring me up?"

The attendant looked a little bewildered by my sudden demands and how quickly I was talking, but he moved to do as I asked.

"I'd also like to pay the balance of that lady's layaway. Oh! And also add this to her bag, please." I grabbed a couple Nerf guns from a nearby display, hoping they were good for kids that age—an extra little gift from a girl with elf friends.

I tapped my phone to pay just as the lady hung up and turned back to the counter.

"Thank you, ma'am. That's very generous." The man gave me a genuine smile and turned his eyes to the woman.

I reached out to cover his hand with mine, then put my other finger to my lips in a silent plea for secrecy. He gave me a little nod.

"Merry Christmas," I said.

"Merry Christmas, and a happy new year." He turned to the lady, and I turned to my friends … who were all beaming at me.

"She's back." El nodded.

"Come on." I rushed toward the door, and they followed.

I chanced one quick look behind me. The lady was crying, staring in disbelief at her purchases on the counter before her.

My heart felt warm and fuzzy.

THE SNOW GLOBE

Once we'd moved away from the store's front entrance, Tin pulled me to a stop, and they all crowded in.

"What happened in there, Sadie?" Elvis asked.

I shrugged. "I just remembered what Christmas is really about."

"But what about all those presents for your family?" Tin frowned.

"I was consumed by material stuff. I'd forgotten it's not about how much you spend or what brand name you're buying. It's about *giving*. And that's more about what's in your heart than what's in your wallet."

"Knew you'd get there in the end." Max smiled, his hands in his pockets. They all shared amused, knowing looks.

"You guys knew I was going off the rails?" I chided. "Why'd you play along and let me lose my shit? Why didn't you rein me in? We don't exactly have time for this."

"It's one of those things you have to realize on your own." El shrugged.

"And we weren't worried," Tin added. "We knew you'd get there."

"Well, I had some help." I smiled at Max. "Thank you. And thank you all for putting up with me, and for standing up for me with that dick Brian, and for being patient even though I nearly ruined Christmas."

"You didn't ruin anything. You saved it." Max pulled the snow globe out of Tin's pocket and held it up for us all to see.

It was now constantly glowing, the staggeringly detailed scene inside positively alive. The Christmas tree forest was vibrant and verdant; the little cottage was lit up from the inside, the chimney smoking; and the sleigh in front was shiny red—there was even a little blanket on the seat. The snow wasn't swirling around and settling in fat chunks the way it did in other snow globes. It was falling from the "sky"—just appearing at the top of the globe and drifting down to kiss the tops of the trees, the roof of the cottage, the soft ground.

"Now we're in business." Tin rubbed his hands together.

"Fully charged, baby!" El held his fist out, and Tin bumped it. He did the same to Max, then me.

"Great job, Sadie." Max kissed me on the cheek, and I smiled, mumbling thanks at the ground.

On the bit of sidewalk in the middle of our little group, magic began to swirl. My eyes widened, and we all took a small step back. Uncertain, I looked around at the elves, but they all had happy smiles on their faces, so at least I knew that whatever was happening wasn't dangerous.

This magic was just as brilliant and sparkling as the white, red, and gold magic I'd seen from them, but it didn't have a particular color. It was kind of iridescent, glinting with every color imaginable all at once. Mesmerizing.

As the glittering, swirling magic faded, a form became clear in the middle of the flurry.

"Cutting it close, you three." The Elf propped her hands on her hips and eyed El, Tin, and Max with an amused look.

At three feet tall, with pointed ears and pointed shoes that matched her elaborately embroidered green outfit, she was much closer to what I'd thought Christmas elves looked like before I met the three tall, sexy ones who had taken me on an adventure all over the city. Her big eyes seemed to sparkle permanently, and she was somehow both childlike and old and wise looking at the same time.

"Hey, Shinny." Tin stepped forward first, giving her a hug. As the others followed suit, I looked around us. People walking out of the department store weaved around our odd little group, but no one was sparing us a glance. It was as if having a magical being appear out of thin air in a cloud of glitter were totally normal. Of course no one had seen her—they probably still couldn't.

"Sadie."

At the sound of my name pronounced in her high yet distinguished voice, I turned back to face her. She was looking right up at me, a knowing smile on her face.

"Hello. So nice to meet you." I extended my hand, and she shook it with her small one. Her hand felt warm, and my palm tingled pleasantly when she pulled away.

"That was touch and go for a while there, but I'm glad you got it in the end," she said.

"Oh, thanks." I cleared my throat, feeling awkward for nearly derailing something so important.

"None of that now," she chided, even wagging her finger up at me. "No harm, no foul. But you've left yourselves with no time to get back to the sleigh."

"Oh, shit." I checked my watch. It was quarter to midnight. There was no longer a crowd on the street, just the last few shoppers heading home. The skating rink and Christmas market were closed, and the store was getting ready to close too. The city was finally winding down, ready to go to sleep and greet Christmas in the morning.

But they might be waking up to nothing under their trees. We'd never make it back to my apartment by midnight, and I had no idea how long El needed to fix the issue with the sleigh.

My shoulders slumped. We'd failed after all.

I looked up to say sorry to the guys, but they didn't look worried in the slightest. The three of them stood with their hands in their pockets, easy smiles on their faces, their postures relaxed.

"Psst." Shinny nudged me with her elbow and winked, then stage-whispered, "That's why I'm here. Thought I might give you one last push to get the job done."

Without waiting for any kind of response, she held her hands out at her sides, palms up, and her iridescent magic appeared again. This time, it swirled around all of us.

The magic tingled a little as it flitted over my skin, making the loose hair at my temples flutter. I started to feel an odd kind of weightlessness, exhilarating and a little disconcerting at the same time. Tin was the closest, so I grabbed on to his arm with both hands and plastered myself to his side.

He chuckled and wrapped his free arm around my shoulders, drawing me into his chest. Over his shoulder, I watched the glittering magic intensify until the city street completely disappeared from view.

And then we were back where we started—in the dingy parking lot at the back of my building—as the magic once again faded to nothing.

"Good luck!" Shinny's voice floated on the breeze, disappearing with the last sparks of magic.

I slowly backed out of Tin's embrace, clutching my stomach and holding on to his arm with one hand. That particular mode of transport was certainly efficient, but it had left me feeling a bit queasy.

"You OK, Sadie?" Max asked.

"It's best not to think about it too hard." El stepped forward. "It'll only make the nausea worse. Tin?"

He held his hand out, and Tin reached into his pocket to hand him the globe.

With another deep breath of icy air, I released Tin's arm. We were standing right by the askew dumpsters at the back of the lot, the one dim streetlight flickering in and out.

Max helped El pull the tarp back, revealing the sleigh, and El immediately hunched down at the back of it. He fiddled around for several minutes while the three of us waited patiently. After a series of clangs, whirrs, and dings from the sleigh and a string of grunts, curses, and growls from El, he straightened up with a satisfied hum and flashed us a grin, wiping his hands with the greasy rag.

We came around the side of the sleigh to look. The engine—if I could call it that—looked like something between a steampunk engine and a fantastical abstract painting, but it was all bright and glimmering. Cogs, wheels, pipes, and steaming things were somehow connected to all manner of twisted, glittering parts in gold, silver, and red. In the middle of it all sat the snow globe. The elaborately carved base was slotted into its spot, and the glowing ball protruded from between a bullhorn-looking thing emitting shimmery green steam and something that looked like a metallic candy cane.

I had no idea what any of it was or what it did.

After staring at it for a few moments, I scratched my head and looked around at the guys. "What now?"

"We need to jump-start it," El said.

Max reached into his coat and pulled out the pouch he'd been using to collect Christmassy items from all the places we'd visited. He tugged the drawstring open. "Here we go."

Tin reached over and pulled out the little mitten El had collected at the Christmas concert, then held it out as if offering it to the sleigh engine. Once it was in the light of the snow globe, the glow intensified, iridescent Christmas magic sparkled and swirled, and then the mitten was gone—for lack of a better explanation, sucked into the globe.

Max passed him the program with all the carols in it, and Tin repeated the process—glow, magic swirl, gone. The pine tree sprig and tuft of reindeer fur went next, and I smiled, remembering how soft and warm the fur had felt under my hand as I stroked it in the woods.

The little bells jingled as Max pulled out the reindeer ears from the party and passed them to Tin. The cookies went next, but not before Tin took a sneaky little bite, making me laugh.

An icy gust of wind had me pulling El's coat tighter across my body, but my fascination with this process helped me ignore the cold for the most part.

El rubbed the top of my arm for warmth as he stepped forward and twisted his hand over the top of the pouch. His golden magic sparkled and drew out a swirling stream of the Christmas faery's green glitter, sending it sailing into the snow globe.

I watched with wide eyes and a mesmerized smile pulling at my lips. We were all silent during this process—something about it felt special, as if it demanded a certain level of quiet reverence.

"It's empty." Max broke the silence, holding the pouch upside down and shaking it before tucking it away.

"Oh! Here!" Tin snapped his fingers and reached into the inside pocket of his coat to pull out a length of red-and-white-striped wrapping ribbon. He added it to the globe.

"That's right." Max smiled and pulled out the pebble Snowie had given us, adding that too.

We all turned to El. He shoved his hand into the pocket of his pants and pulled out a flat, round object, about six inches in diameter.

I burst out laughing. "Is that the automatic floss dispenser?"

"Yep." He grinned, looking satisfied with himself. "It may not be that traditional, but useless gifts have become a part of Christmas for many people." He flicked his wrist, throwing the item into the glow. The globe sparkled with magic and accepted his offering.

"Did you steal that?" I asked through residual laughter.

"Nope. I paid for it fair and square." He rolled his shoulders back, the picture of confidence.

I shook my head.

"Can't believe you paid money for that," Tin teased.

"Guys, it's not starting up." Max frowned. "Why isn't it starting up?"

We all gave our full attention to the fantastical contraption. I had no idea what I was looking at, but it was glowing and humming, as if it was trying to do something.

El leaned over to fiddle with a few parts, then straightened up again. "It's super close. Just needs one tiny bit more to get it going, I think. Anyone got anything else we can add?"

He looked around at us. Tin and Max were starting to look worried.

"Oh!" I snapped my fingers as I remembered the mistletoe. Tin had slid it into my hair with a gentle kiss just before we were chased out of Monica's work party.

I pulled it out and twirled it between my fingers, then twisted to give El a peck on the lips. He smiled, the glint in his eye telling me he was remembering the fun we'd had in that office just as well as I was.

Stepping forward toward the sleigh, I gave Tin a kiss too.

"I told you there was more than one way to feel cheerful." He grinned, and I couldn't help laughing as I added the mistletoe to the globe.

Just as the green sprig disappeared in a swirl of sparkling magic, a fat white flake landed on the back of my hand.

I gasped and looked up. The sky was dark, my breath misted in the freezing air, and it had finally started to snow.

White flakes fell from the sky, and even though it was technically bits of ice floating down toward us, my heart felt warmer. I knew it would be snowing where my parents lived, where my whole family was gathered at this very moment. The kids would be in bed by now, as well as most of the adults, but I knew my dad and a few of my aunts and cousins would still be sitting around the fire, sipping on mulled wine and chatting quietly, the tree lit up in the corner. It made me feel closer to them, even though I couldn't be there.

An arm circled my waist from behind, and a hard chest pressed against my back. I craned my neck to see El holding me, his face tipped up to the sky just like mine.

Max stepped up on my right and gently leaned into my side, and Tin appeared at my left. I took Tin's hand, twining my fingers with his, and laid my head on Max's shoulder.

For a brief moment, we all just looked up to the sky, watching the falling snow envelop the world around us in white and silence.

A humming noise brought our attention back down. Magic rippled from the snow globe and spread over the whole sleigh, pulsing just once, and then slowly, the sleigh started to float, perfectly level with the ground.

As the sleigh rose, my heart fell. I hadn't known it was possible to feel so happy and so sad at the same time. I was overjoyed that we'd succeeded, that I'd been able to help three magical Christmas elves fix their sleigh, that kids would get their presents the next morning. But I was crestfallen that they were about to leave.

I'd have to go back up to my sad, lonely apartment and spend the rest of the night alone after all. Would I ever even see them again? Did elves have cell phones? Would they even want to give me their numbers?

With the rejuvenation of the sleigh, the guys sprang into action. Max pulled his tablet out, tapping at it and staring intently at the screen. El fiddled with the engine, then closed the lid as Tin folded up the tarp. Once they'd both jumped inside, El started flicking switches and turning knobs on a complicated-looking control panel.

Only Max still stood on the ground as the sleigh hovered a foot in the air—I couldn't even give El and Tin a goodbye kiss.

I knew it was childish and probably selfish, but I didn't want them to leave. I wasn't ready to say goodbye.

THE SNOW

"All right! Let's jingle bell rock and roll." Max leaned around me to toss the tablet onto the seat. Tin had taken his coat off and was rummaging in the back, straightening things that had fallen askew when they'd crashed.

Max didn't even look at me as he spoke—none of them did, absorbed as they were in the task of getting the sleigh moving.

I knew they were focused and committed to their jobs, but was Max really going to brush past me and jump into the sleigh as if I didn't exist? Were none of them even going to look at me or wave goodbye? Were they really going to leave just like that?

Tears stung the backs of my eyes, and I looked down, focusing on the snow starting to coat the ground. I couldn't watch them leave me without so much as a word.

Strong hands circled my waist, and I let out a surprised squeak as Max lifted me into the sleigh. El pulled me down next to him, and I had to lift the tablet out of the way as he pulled me to his side. Max jumped in, took off his coat, flung it at Tin's head, and plonked down next to me, grabbing the tablet out of my hands.

"Top-secret Christmas information here. Elf eyes only." He winked and started poking the screen again.

I just blinked at him, my mouth hanging slightly open. I'd been convinced I was about to be left behind, sad and lonely, in the shady parking area behind my shitty apartment building, but here I was, sitting in the middle of an actual fucking sleigh.

"You didn't think we'd leave you behind, did you, Sadie?" El draped an arm over the back of the seat and flashed me an amused smile.

I cleared my throat. "No?" It came out like a question. I didn't want to lie to them, but I also didn't want them to know how quick I'd been to assume the worst.

Tin leaned over the back of the seat and planted a kiss on my cheek. "We'd never just leave you, baby. No way we'd let you put in so much time and effort and not let you see the results. Also, we're *gentlemen* elves—we don't hit it and quit it."

That made me chuckle, and I relaxed into the seat. It was the softest black leather, trimmed in red, and the shiny dark green dash and controls matched the sleek exterior. The knobs, buttons, and displays lit up and sparkled like Christmas lights.

As I took it all in, I realized I was boiling in El's coat. Frowning, I took it off, and Tin pulled it out of my hands to tuck in a corner with the others.

"How is it so warm?" I asked, looking around. The sleigh was modern and really sleek looking, but the top was completely open. Although now that I looked up, I could see the snow wasn't reaching our heads. It just melted away about a foot above El's red hair.

"Magic." El shrugged. "It looks open, like a proper sleigh, but there's a domelike shape over the top of it, keeping us warm and safe from snow, rain, and birds."

"What about planes?" I asked.

"The navigation system picks them up. We fly lower than most commercial aircraft anyway, and humans can't normally see us, remember? There hasn't been a run-in with a plane since..." He scrunched his face up, thinking hard.

"Nineteen sixty-four," Max supplied.

"Right. Ready?" El flashed me a smile, and a bubble of excitement made me squirm and bounce in my seat like a kid.

He pressed a few more buttons, pushed a lever, and then we were *flying*. We lifted off the ground so smoothly my stomach didn't even drop. The sleigh glided over the city, El maneuvering it expertly with a lever that seemed to control altitude and a small oval-shaped steering wheel.

I looked up to watch the snow falling softly, then leaned over Max to see the lights of houses and buildings whoosh by. Then I looked to the sides, the front, the back, watching the horizon, the twinkling lights of the coastline.

"Would you stop wriggling around?" Tin chuckled. "You're gonna throw us off course, and we'll crash again."

"Shit." I planted my feet and sat on my hands, my eyes going wide.

"He's just teasing." Max smacked Tin on the back of the head. "It's almost impossible to make these things crash. Now, let's get to work."

"Good thing we'd finished most of the city before we crashed," El said.

"That means the most densely populated areas are done," Max explained, his face back in the tablet.

"What? How?" I frowned. It was barely six when they crashed. "Wouldn't people have been awake?"

"Yes, but *magic*!" Max leaned in and whispered the word as if it were a secret, chuckling. "We can't start delivering until the sun has set and it's officially nighttime, but obviously not everyone goes to bed that early. So the presents delivered before the occupants are asleep remain invisible."

"Yeah, it's a similar kind of magic to what cloaks the sleigh," El added.

"But what about the people who stay up all night? Do they just not get presents?"

"At some point, no one is watching the tree. Even if it's just for a moment," Tin called from the back.

I wanted to ask more questions, but we'd started flying closer to the ground.

The sleigh slowed, hovering just above the roofline of a busy street filled with tightly packed townhouses. We were on the outskirts of the city, in a much better area than the one I lived in.

Tin swung his arms at the pile of presents in the back—or rather *piles and piles*, some in sacks, some stacked so high I couldn't believe they weren't falling out of the sleigh, so many presents they seemed endless. The amount of room back there was definitely a magical situation, because the sleigh was *not* that size from the outside. Magic swirled from his hands—brilliant, shimmery white magic that twirled around the gifts. Some of the items disappeared, and tendrils of magic went shooting to every house on the street, disappearing inside.

It happened in a matter of seconds, and before I could blink, we were on to the next street. El steered with confidence; Max kept an eye on everything, ticking things off a long list; and Tin practically danced around in the back, flinging magic and presents all over the place.

Between Christmas magic making everything go super fast and the guys' proficiency, we completed an entire neighborhood in under ten minutes.

"This is incredible," I breathed.

I pulled my boots off and crossed my legs on the seat, watching them work and taking in the stunning views from the comfort of the warm sleigh. After a while, something occurred to me.

"Hey, what about that whole chimney thing?" I asked. "Obviously all the presents are being delivered by magic. I mean, you guys don't even get out of the sleigh. Did Santa ever go down chimneys?"

They all laughed, but it was El who answered, his eyes on the horizon. "Nah. Santa always did it with magic. But we do fly pretty close to the rooftops, and he wasn't always kept invisible to the humans. Plus, in the nineteenth century there was this notorious thief in Europe who would climb down chimneys to access wealthy people's homes. Somewhere along the way, the stories got crossed, and I think that's where that comes from."

"Huh." I tilted my head. "What about the cookies?"

"There's no way one man could eat that much," Tin answered as he swirled more magic, delivering a continuous stream of presents as the sleigh flew through the sky. "But we do take some from time to time—the ones that look good, homemade."

I turned to look at him. "How can you tell from out here?"

He winked at me. "I told you I was in charge of snacks, right?"

"That doesn't actually answer my question." I rolled my eyes, smiling, but turned back to the front.

Tin looked so damn cute, slinging magic, his T-shirt stretching over his chest as he worked. El was the picture of cool, one hand on the steering wheel, the corded muscle in his forearm dancing with every slight movement while his other arm rested on the seat behind me. Max was the quietest, constantly prodding his tablet. In his defense, it was hard to get a word in edgewise with Tin and El.

He looked so handsome, his profile strong, his broad shoulders just begging to be gripped ...

I bit my bottom lip and shifted on my seat. I'd gotten what I wanted, and more, with Tin and El, but Max and I still had unfinished business. Business my body was ready to get back to if the building pressure between my legs was anything to go by. But now wasn't really the best time ... was it?

I leaned into El's side, and he wrapped his free arm around my waist. Trailing my fingers through his soft auburn hair, I whispered in his ear, "I have a question."

He hummed, keeping his eyes ahead.

"What's Max doing exactly?"

The corner of his mouth twitched. He flicked me a quick, amused look before leaning his head to the side to whisper, "Keeping an eye on progress, ticking off the list. Nothing that he can't be distracted from for a while."

I was trying to be subtle, but El obviously knew exactly what I had on my dirty mind. I gave him a kiss on the neck, and he squeezed my waist before I pulled away to face Max.

I tucked my legs under me, my knees pressing up against the side of Max's thigh, and propped my head on my hand, watching him.

After a few moments, his lips pulled into a smile, and he glanced in my direction. "Yes, Sadie?"

"Nothing." I shrugged, pitching my voice low. "I just like watching you work. You look so sexy." I lifted my head and stroked the back of his neck with the tips of my fingers, dipping them under the collar of his T-shirt.

His smile fell, and he swallowed, that adorable blush creeping up his cheeks. It was so cute how he could be confident and crack dirty jokes when we were in the moment, rubbing up on each other, yet be so bashful too.

"Thanks." He kept his eyes on the tablet but stopped tapping and scrolling. I had his full attention.

I scratched the back of his neck with my nails and leaned in to whisper in his ear, "I want to finish what we started in the store earlier."

Pressing my boobs against his arm, I nipped the shell of his ear before trailing kisses down his neck. His pulse thudded under my lips as he tilted his head, giving me better access.

His defined chest started to rise and fall more rapidly as his breathing shallowed. The tablet was quickly abandoned in a nook next to the seat, and then his hand was at my cheek, his gentle fingers nudging my face up so he could kiss me.

The first time we kissed in the store, we were hesitant, unsure, slow. This time, when we kissed, it was *instant heat*. His tongue demanded entry, and I allowed it willingly, sighing against him.

He angled his body more toward mine as we kissed, his hands on me making me feel as if I were soaring even higher than the sleigh in the sky.

I trailed my hand down his front, taking my time to feel the hard planes of his body under the soft white cotton. When I reached his pants, I fumbled to undo them, and he dropped his hand down to help me. We got in each other's way, our fingers bumping as we smiled against each other's mouths, but eventually we got the fly open.

I didn't waste any time, reaching into his briefs and wrapping my hand around his length. He was so hard—silk covered steel. As I stroked him, Max moaned and licked his lips, his warm breath washing over my face. His eyes were hooded as he watched what my hand was doing in his lap, his wet, plump lips parted.

I pushed the fabric of his underwear down, exposing his engorged length, giving him a better view. After another few strokes, I scooted back a bit and leaned down to take him into my mouth.

Three groans sounded from around me. In such close quarters, it was no wonder we had an audience. The thought of Tin and El watching as I licked and sucked Max, taking him deeper into my mouth, sent a thrill of desire shooting down my spine.

I moaned around him, and he grunted, threading his fingers into my hair, messing up my ponytail.

The bench seat was roomy when the three of us were sitting on it. But with me perched sideways with my face in Max's lap, my feet ended up pressed against El's thigh, leaving my ass in the air.

I was hoping El might take it as an invitation and was more than pleased when he reached out and stroked me over the fabric.

El didn't mess around, dragging his hand up over the curve of my ass and grabbing the edge of my tights. I felt the tug of another hand and knew Tin was helping him. They worked together until my tights and underwear were at my knees, my skirt pushed up around my waist and my ass and pussy totally exposed.

"Fuck." El groaned as he stroked me again, his fingers spreading the moisture.

"So beautiful," Tin breathed, dragging a hand down my back and squeezing my ass. Then they were both touching me.

I was moaning on every breath, my mouth on Max's cock messy and uneven now that I was lost in my own pleasure. Two hands played with me between my legs—sliding in and out, rubbing, teasing, thrusting—as I struggled to focus on giving Max a blowjob.

"Are you wet, Sadie?" Max asked, his voice strained and gravelly.

I released him from my mouth and looked up. "Yes."

"She's fucking soaked," El added.

"Are you?" Max kept his gaze on me, his chest heaving. "Are you soaked for us? You like having all our hands on you?"

"Fuck." I had to take a breath before I could answer properly—the hands between my legs were moving faster, rubbing harder. "Yes. I'm dripping wet for you. I like having you all touch me. I like having you all watch me. And when we have more room than this, I want all of you at the same time."

Tin cursed under his breath, making incoherent sounds at my naughty words.

Max's mouth curved up in a little grin, his eyes glinting. He liked that. *A lot.*

"Stop," he ordered, and the hands between my legs immediately pulled away. I whimpered and frowned at him before I could stop myself.

"Your next orgasm is mine," Max said, pushing his pants and underwear down his legs. He snapped his fingers, and a condom appeared in a swirl of red magic. He slid it down his length as I sat up and pulled my tights off the rest of the way.

Max took my hand and drew me toward him, maneuvering me with a strong, confident hold on my hips until I was straddling his lap but facing away from him.

Out of the corner of my eye, I could see El. He was no longer focused on flying the sleigh—he wasn't even looking ahead. He was angled toward us, one leg up on the bench seat, his hand slowly stroking the bulge in his pants.

For a split second, I worried we would crash, but then I realized we weren't moving. Facing the front, I could see for miles around, and all I saw were stars and soft hills of white. El had parked us above the clouds, and everything around us was so still—beautiful—as the night sky twinkled.

I paused for a moment, momentarily mesmerized by the view.

Before I could lower myself onto Max's thighs, his cock appeared between my legs. He held it firmly at the base and slid it back and forth over my folds, making me moan and slap my hand on the dash for balance.

His hand on my hip tugged, and then he was sliding into me. I impaled myself completely on his hardness in one go, and we both moaned. The feeling of fullness, the angle, the exhilaration of hovering above the clouds made for a heady cocktail in my body, and I was panting within seconds. My core clenched around him, and I started to rock my hips.

"Take her dress off, Max. Please," Tin pleaded, his voice sounding very close. I looked over my shoulder to find him leaning on the back of the seat right next to us, one arm half-hidden behind the backrest and moving in a steady rhythm. El had his perfect, straight dick out too; he stroked it slowly as he watched my hips gyrate.

Max took pity on them and gripped the bottom of my dress. I straightened up and lifted my arms so he could take it off and fling it over his shoulder.

Instead of letting me lean forward again, Max captured my shoulder with one hand while the other splayed over my belly, holding me flush against his chest.

I was in nothing but a bra. The fabric—and the way my back was arched—pushed my tits forward and up, creating perfect cleavage, if I did say so myself. It was one of my own designs, a green-and-white candy cane pattern for the straps with white cups and delicate green trim, finished off with a little green bow between the cups.

"You have the most perfect tits." El groaned, watching them bounce as I ground myself on Max.

"And the bra," Tin added. "Christmas wet dream."

Max moved his hand down from my shoulder to my breast,

squeezing it and pushing it up. I arched into his touch, reaching an arm over my head to grip the back of the seat. I looked straight up at the stars above us, completely lost in the sensations coursing through my body.

"That's it." Max's breath was hot in my ear, panting and rough as he bucked his hips under me. "Ride me deep, baby."

With one hand still at my breast, he trailed the other down and began to stroke my clit.

I cried out and started riding him harder. Between his thick length rubbing me deep inside and his strong fingers touching me between my legs, it wasn't long before my first orgasm washed over me. It burst through my body, making me see more stars than the ones I was already looking at.

Max kept rubbing me until I stopped crying out, but he didn't give me time to recover. He pushed my shoulders forward until I was sitting up and unclasped my bra, taking it off and flinging it behind him. Then, with a firm hand between my shoulder blades, he maneuvered me until I had both hands propped up on the dash of the sleigh. My back was arched, my tits hanging heavy, and I was already moaning at the new angle.

I looked between us, licking my lips at the sight of where we were joined.

Max gripped my ponytail and tugged, denying me the view and making me arch more, my neck stretched.

"OK?" Max asked, stilling completely.

"Uh-huh, yes, fuck me, Max," I managed to say between panting breaths.

The other two groaned at my dirty words, and Max didn't need another invitation.

With one hand fisted in my hair and the other gripping my hip almost painfully, he guided our movements.

I had to work my thighs to slide up and down his cock, but he thrust up every time I lowered myself onto him, creating a deep, hard, intense rhythm.

The sounds of all four of us moaning and grunting mingled in the night, driving my pleasure higher.

Max pounded into me and came with a drawn-out groan, releasing my hair and pressing his chest flush with my back as he rode it out. The intense way he rolled his hips into me—his cock hitting a spot deep inside—coupled with the sudden appearance of Tin's hands at my breasts had me crying out again.

Tin pinched my nipples, then gripped my tits, kneading them gently as my second orgasm washed through me, wave after wave of pleasure sending tingles across my skin.

I leaned forward farther, forcing Tin to release my breasts, and rested my head on my arms as I tried to catch my breath.

Eventually, I pushed myself up into a sitting position. El was reclined against the other side of the sleigh, his cock still out, one arm thrown over his eyes as his chest heaved. His T-shirt was pushed up, revealing his cut abs and the mess he'd made on them.

A glance over my shoulder told me Tin was in a similar position, but he was flashing me a cheeky grin and had already cleaned himself up.

A light slap at my thigh brought my attention back to Max.

"Up," he commanded, then kissed the back of my neck. "That was a fun interlude, but we are so far behind now. We gotta haul ass."

"But what an ass," Tin called from the back, making us all laugh as I lifted myself off Max's softening dick. Hopefully I hadn't fixed the power core only to make it impossible for them to finish their deliveries with my greedy sexual needs.

THE CHRISTMAS TREE

Like a well-oiled machine, the guys straightened their clothing, cleaned up, and got back to work. I was still pulling my dress over my head when El started the sleigh back into motion and began guiding it down through the clouds.

Once we cleared the cloud layer, the guys picked up the pace, and I stayed out of their way as much as possible while sitting in the middle of them. I helped where I could, passing a wayward present to Tin, pointing out an area of the city to El so he could navigate a little better, and just leaning on Max's shoulder, who was so on top of it he didn't need help with anything. I stayed silent for the most part, letting them concentrate and trying to ignore the nervous energy rising in my gut.

"Are we going to make it?" I asked, chewing on my bottom lip. A faint purple glow was starting to light the sky.

"Yeah, we got this." Max gave me a confident smile, and I allowed myself to relax a little.

"Last one." El slowed the sleigh above a curving suburban street. Snow coated the rooftops and sidewalks, the pristine powder untouched in the night.

"Piece of fruitcake." Tin grinned, throwing out his white magic and delivering dozens of presents to the neighborhood in one go.

As the horizon continued to lighten, the guys all high-fived and then turned to me for victory kisses, making me giggle at their enthusiasm.

When they'd all settled back into their spots, I wondered how long it would take to get back to my apartment—how much more time I had with them before they had to drop me off. If we'd been driving, it would have taken at least an hour through this weather, but we were flying, so it would probably be a lot faster. What would they do once they took me home? Would they go back to the North Pole? Celebrate? Sleep?

"All right. One last stop." Max settled back in his seat as El nodded and took off again.

"What?" I looked between them. "I thought that was the last delivery."

"It was." Tin leaned over the back of the seat, nuzzling his nose in my hair. "Our job is done, just in the nick of time. We've delivered all the presents. We just have one more special delivery to do."

"What is it?" I asked.

"Look." El nodded to the front of the sleigh.

I dragged my attention away from Tin—he was starting to place soft kisses on my neck—to look around.

El lowered the sleigh down past the rooftops, much lower than he'd been doing all night. As it neared the ground and "parked" in the middle of the street, the surroundings started to look familiar.

It was still snowing softly, fine flakes gently piling on top of each other to create a blanket of white on the quiet suburban street. The predawn glow, darkened by the heavy clouds, cast everything in a gray light.

I covered my mouth with my hands as tears welled in my eyes.

There was the Thompsons' yard, where I'd had my first crash while learning to ride my bike without training wheels. I could just see the corner where Bobby Nichols had given me my first kiss as he walked me home from the movies. And right there, right in front of me, was my parents' house—the tall spruce in the yard, the winding path to the front steps I knew was beneath the snow, the wide front porch, the bright red mailbox my mom had insisted on when the old one was taken out by rowdy teens with baseball bats, even though it didn't match the gray and white of the rest of the house at all. There were too many memories in the front yard to name.

"You brought me home?" I whispered as I wiped the moisture from under my eyes.

"For Christmas." Tin rested his chin on my shoulder, and I leaned my head against his as we stared at my childhood home.

"This is…" I had no words. I'd expected them to just boot me out of the sleigh as they sailed past the city on their way back to the North Pole. Perhaps I wasn't giving them enough credit, but I'd only just met these men a few hours ago—I didn't want to assume anything.

The fact that they'd remembered how badly I wanted to be home for Christmas was beyond heartwarming.

"Get in there before the sun comes up fully." El nodded to my parents' place. "The last delivery must be made before sunrise."

"Merry Christmas, Sadie." Max's voice was low and melancholy, but his gentle smile was genuine as he squeezed my hand.

I knew this had to be hard for them. Bringing me to my family on a picturesque street on a perfect Christmas morning. I knew they were thinking about things they never had or things they'd lost too soon. They'd put my happiness first, and I couldn't think of a better example of selfless giving—from the heart and soul.

El, Max, and Tin were perfect for what they did. Their stories may have been tinged with sadness, but they knew how to bring joy like no one's business.

I took a breath and swallowed around the lump in my throat. "Thank you. All of you. Thank you so much for bringing me to my family. And for taking me along for this adventure. I'll never forget it. Merry Christmas."

I twisted to face Tin over the back of the seat and wrapped my arms around his neck, giving him a tight hug and a soft kiss. He flashed me one of his infectious grins, and his eyes glinted with white magic as I pulled away.

I launched myself at Max next, and he pulled me into his lap, holding me against his chest as he gave me a firm, lingering kiss. I cupped his cheek and stared into his eyes, mesmerized by the spark of red magic as he sighed.

El was facing the front, a slight frown creasing his brow, his long fingers picking at the bottom of the steering wheel. I scooted over to his side and rested my chin on his shoulder, giving him a kiss on the cheek.

He sighed but didn't shrug me off—he lifted one arm and wrapped it around my shoulders. I took it as my in and climbed into his lap, straddling him. I had to grip his face to make him look at me. When his eyes finally connected with mine, there was frustration and sadness in them.

"What's wrong?" I asked, keeping it simple. The sun was nearly fully up—we were running out of time.

He gripped my hips, looking uncertain for a moment, then sighed again and rolled his eyes. "I don't want you to leave. But I also want you to see your family for Christmas. I'm ... *conflicted.*"

In answer, I pressed my lips to his. Underneath all the sarcasm and bravado, he was such a sweet man. They all just wanted to be loved, and who couldn't relate to that?

As soon as my lips met El's, he deepened the kiss, demanding more, banding his arms around my back and forcing my chest flush with his. I gave him what he wanted, kissing him deeply and holding him tightly. When I started to consider blowing off my family for another round of fun in the sleigh, I pulled away.

"You're killing me." I groaned, and he flashed me a grin, calling up his dimples.

"Just don't want you to forget us." He gave me one last kiss on the lips, that glint of green magic in his eyes.

"I could never forget you, El. I'll always remember this night and all of you. I promise." I chewed on my lip, uncertain how to phrase the next question. "Am I ... will we ... uh, will I ever see you again?"

"Would you like to?" Max asked from behind me while at the same time Tin announced, "Fuck yeah, you will," and El squeezed my waist and gave me a serious "Yes."

I grinned and decided to leave it at that. They wanted to see me again, and on this crazy night, I was choosing to have faith they would figure out how when the time was right. I resisted the urge to ask about phone numbers—they knew where I lived. They'd find me.

"OK. Time to go." I patted El on the shoulder, and he stood with me in his arms. The muscles in his chest, arms, and back strained as he lifted me over the edge of the sleigh and deposited me on the street.

Immediately, I wrapped my arms around my middle. Now that I was outside the sleigh's warm, protective magic, I was freezing.

I flashed them one more smile and waved before rushing across the yard to my parents' place.

Just as I ran up the steps onto the porch, a flash of Christmas magic came sailing past my head. It was Tin's brilliant white, shimmering better than fresh snow in sunshine, but it was tinged with Max's red and El's gold as well. It flashed past me and disappeared as it reached the front door, jostling the elaborate wreath.

I turned on my heel, the question at the tip of my tongue, but they were already gone. Two streaks of iridescent Elf magic curved up into the sky, giving the impression of sleigh tracks in the air, but they were already fading.

The light just inside the front door came on, casting yellow beams across the porch, and I turned back to the house before I could wonder anymore about what the guys had done with their magic.

The door opened, and my dad nearly barreled into me.

"Whoa!" He jumped back and dropped his gloves, one hand flying to his chest. He was bundled up in a puffy jacket and boots, and his blond hair—same shade as mine but peppered with gray—poked out of the bottom of a bright red beanie. The giant white pom-pom on top bounced as he jumped, making me laugh.

"Sadie?" He placed his hands on my shoulders. "You scared me half to death."

"Sorry, Dad." I stomped my feet. "Can we go back inside? It's freezing."

"Shit. Of course." He pulled me into the house and closed the door. The warmth of central heating almost immediately had me sighing and dropping my tense shoulders.

I took my boots off as my dad removed all his extra layers.

"What are you doing up so early, Dad?" When I was younger, my parents used to get up early with me to open presents around the tree. But now that we were all grown, we normally spent the morning sleeping off the mulled wine from Christmas Eve dinner, then gathered around the tree with the extended family later in the day.

"I was coming to get you." He shrugged as he hung up his coat.

I paused on my way to the living room and turned to face him, bugging my eyes out. "Dad. It's been snowing. That's at least a three-hour drive there in this weather and then *another* three hours back."

"Well, I didn't know it was gonna bloody snow, did I?" He propped his hands on his hips but smiled. "Didn't want you to miss Christmas."

I sighed and went in for a hug, squeezing him tightly around the middle. "That's really sweet, old man."

"Who you calling old?" he chastised, but he rocked me from side to side. "Good to have you home, kid."

"Who you calling kid?" I laughed as I pulled away, surreptitiously wiping at the moisture under my eyes.

"You'll always be my kid. Now, come into the kitchen so your old man can make you a peppermint hot chocolate."

He took off without waiting for a response, and I followed him into the living room.

As I passed the Christmas tree in the corner, its twinkle lights glowing in the dark room, I paused. Dad started clanging around the kitchen—opening cupboards, moving pots and pans—as I inched closer to the tree and bent down to get a closer look.

"Those sneaky, sexy bastards..." I mumbled under my breath, a slow smile pulling at my lips.

Sitting under the tree, in among all the other gifts, were the presents that had been stolen out of my car. They'd used their Christmas magic to get my gifts back from whatever lowlife had taken them. Or maybe they were all new gifts—it didn't matter. What mattered was that those three had once again shown me how kind and thoughtful they were.

"Do you know where your mom put the little pot?" Dad called from the kitchen. "I could've sworn I saw her using it yesterday when she..."

I chuckled and joined him in the kitchen. "I haven't lived here in six years. I haven't been here in months, Dad. How would I know where Mom put anything?"

"Aha!" He straightened up from the corner cupboard he'd been rummaging through and held up the little pot with a black handle triumphantly.

I lowered myself onto the stool at the island. The kitchen was timber with granite countertops—earthy and welcoming like the rest of the house—and like the rest of the house, it was decorated with garlands and lights, holiday-themed tea towels and aprons hanging off the oven door.

"Now, what the hell were you doing outside without a coat?" Dad asked as he started making the hot chocolate. "And how did you get here? I thought your car was a goner."

"Can I get some coffee in that as well, please?" I asked through a yawn. I was stalling, avoiding his questions, but I also really wanted some coffee—I hadn't slept all night.

"Sure." He flicked the coffee machine on. "Now answer the questions."

Dammit. "Uh ... the car is a goner. I think. Obviously, I'll have to have someone look at it, but it wouldn't start at all."

"And..." He waved his hand for me to continue.

"And some friends were passing by here, so they were kind enough to give me a lift. They just had some other stops to make first, which is why it took so long. And that's how I ended up standing outside in below-freezing weather—I was just waving goodbye."

"Well, I'm sure as hell glad you found a way to get here." He slid a steaming mug across the bench to me, and I immediately wrapped my hands around it and inhaled, closing my eyes. Chocolate, coffee, and mint hit the back of my nose in a perfect combo of scents. "Who are these friends? Have we met them?"

"No. I only met them recently." I took a sip to avoid saying anything else. "This is excellent, Dad."

He raised his eyebrows over the rim of his own mug as he took a sip. "All right, I'll let you off the hook. But only because you look like shit and I'm glad you're here."

I rolled my eyes. "You mean because you know Mom will ask a million questions and you'll get your answers anyway."

He grinned. "We're a good team like that."

He came to sit on the stool by me, and we sipped our hot chocolate in companionable silence for a short while. Now that he was done banging around the kitchen, the house was quiet, the snow falling outside adding an extra layer of stillness.

"So, how's work? And your apartment? How are things in the city?" Dad asked.

I flashed him a smile and opened my mouth to answer … and the words died in my throat. I'd been about to give him the same response I always gave him on the phone before I changed the subject or hung up—that everything was fine, I loved the city. But I didn't want to lie to him anymore—or myself.

"Actually, Dad, I think I'm over it." My shoulders slumped.

"Over what, sweetheart? What's going on? Is that douchebag Brian still giving you trouble?"

"He has been, but I have a feeling he won't be an issue after tonight." I smiled faintly at the memory of standing up to him, the guys at my back. I'd felt more confident with them there, somehow knowing they'd step in if I needed them to. "No, it's everything. The job, the apartment, being so far away from everyone. I'm just … I'm not happy there."

By the time the hot chocolate was gone, I'd told him all about how my job was OK, but it wasn't what I wanted to be doing; how my apartment was comfortable enough, but I hated not being able to come home for Christmas; how I loved Monica and her friendship, but the thought of getting a corporate job like hers made me want to stab myself in the eye with a pencil.

He listened, asked questions where appropriate, and made all the right comments without judging me.

When I was done, I folded my arms on the counter and dropped my head onto them, groaning. "I'm such a mess. What the fuck am I doing with my life?"

My dad chuckled and stood, taking our mugs to the sink. "That's a tad dramatic. I think you know what you want and how to get it. You're just not going for it."

I thought about that for a while. It was true. I had the business set up. I had dozens of sketchbooks filled with designs. I just wasn't letting myself dive in headfirst and prioritize my dream—I wasn't taking the risk.

Before I could grudgingly admit he was right, the sound of someone coming down the stairs had me turning in my seat.

"Warren?" My mom's groggy voice came from down the hall. "Is that you? I thought you were going to get … Sadie!"

As soon as she rounded the corner and spotted me, she launched herself forward and wrapped me up in a hug, nearly knocking me off my stool.

"Merry Christmas, Mom." I chuckled.

"Oh, merry Christmas, my baby. This is the best gift ever! Warren, make the hot chocolate she likes." She waved in Dad's general direction, her warm brown eyes glued to me and her light brown hair sticking up all over the place.

"We already did that," Dad said.

"Actually, is it OK if I head up and take a shower and a nap before everyone else gets here?" I stood up and stretched.

"Sure, honey. Then you have to tell me how you got here and what's been happening. I missed you *so much*. Oh, but all the rooms are full. Your cousin Mary is in your bed. She hit the eggnog pretty hard last night. But you can snooze on our bed, or the couch in the sunroom if you want. What time is it? Geez, maybe I should get in the shower too..." All this was said while she flitted around the kitchen, got herself a cup of coffee, absentmindedly put on some toast, and removed random items from the fridge—I had no idea what she was planning to do with the ketchup, but Dad picked it up and replaced it before she could close the door.

I smiled as I walked up the stairs. My parents balanced each other perfectly, my dad the calm one, my mom the ball of energy. I hoped the guys and I would find a way to fit so perfectly together.

I paused halfway up the stairs and shook my head before continuing. I'd only just met them, for fuck's sake. I wasn't entirely positive I'd ever even see them again ... I had a feeling Max would put the ketchup back in the fridge for me though.

After a quick shower, I changed into jeans and an oversized sweater with reindeer running across the front, then tried to nap on my parents' bed.

It was no more than half an hour, barely a snooze, before the noise from downstairs became impossible to ignore.

I stretched, put my hair up in a messy bun, and made my way downstairs.

It was ten, but everyone who'd stayed the night was already in the living room. Mugs of coffee and empty plates littered the available surfaces, the floor was covered in ripped wrapping paper, and the younger kids ran around playing with their new toys. The adults would wait until everyone had arrived to do theirs.

I stood in the doorway and managed to take it all in for about thirty seconds before I was spotted.

"Sadie!" my younger cousin Mary yelled at the top of her lungs and rushed up to hug me. She was just finishing college, and we were closest in age out of the cousins, so we'd always been close growing up.

The others all surrounded me, giving me hugs and wishing me merry Christmas. The rest of the family started to arrive one by one. My aunts, uncles, cousins and grandparents—close to forty people— piled into my parents' usually spacious living area. We chatted, played with the kids, and took turns helping my mom and uncle get lunch ready as carols played and the tree sparkled.

Mary was telling me in great detail what she wanted for her birthday—a custom bra and panties set that was making me blush a little, and I'd just had sex with three men in one night—when the doorbell rang again.

I frowned just as Dad popped his head around the corner.

"Who's that?" he asked.

"I don't know. I thought everyone was here. I'll get it." I was closest to the door, so I set my mint-flavored coffee down on a side table and moved to answer it.

THE SHORTBREAD

I did a mental head count as I headed for the door—all my family members were in the living room, even my aunt and uncle who lived on the other side of the country and usually didn't join us for Christmas. Who could possibly be knocking on Christmas Day?

With a slight frown, I opened the door, then gasped and almost took a step back from sheer shock. But my body launched forward of its own accord.

I thought it would be weeks, *months*, before I saw my sexy elves again—I'd half convinced myself I never would. Yet there stood El, Max, and Tin, looking fresh and clean with friendly smiles on their faces.

The smiles widened as I tried to pull them all into a hug at once, making them crouch awkwardly, turn their shoulders, and squish up against one another.

"Sadie." Max chuckled as I released them from my iron grip. "We just saw you a couple of hours ago."

"I know." I kept my voice low, glancing behind me. My cousin was standing very close and eyeing the tall, gorgeous men with a little too much interest, and other family members were rubbernecking as well.

"I just…" I leaned in and practically whispered, "I wasn't sure if…"

"She thought we were gonna ditch her." El stuffed his hands into the pockets of his jeans.

"Wait, what are you wearing?" I finally took a step back to look at them. The black pants and green elf jackets were gone, replaced by everyday, regular clothes.

They were in jeans and boots and warm coats.

"Clothes." El raised his brows and gave me a look as if I were crazy, but I could see the teasing quirk in the corner of his lip.

"Would you like us to take them off?" Tin leaned in and gave me a devious smile.

Naturally, Mary heard that. She threw her head back and laughed, drawing even more attention.

Max was the only one who seemed to take pity on me, saying politely, "We hope you don't mind us popping in. Our plans changed, and we thought we'd come back here. May we come in?"

I opened my mouth to say "fuck yes," but my mom beat me to it, appearing at my back and making me jump. "Of course! Come in out of the cold. Is it still snowing? Shit! We might all get snowed in. Shut that door—you're letting the heat out. Here, let me take your coats. Wow, you're tall!"

She spoke at a million miles an hour, as usual, but the guys handled it good-naturedly, all of them looking amused as she wrangled them out of their plain coats and shuffled them into the living area.

Underneath the coats they were wearing Christmas-themed sweaters that made me smile. Tin was in white with silver snowflakes, Max was in red with a cartoon reindeer, and El was in gold with green wreaths at the neck and sleeves. They looked so fucking cute!

"Introduce us to your friends, Sadie," Mary said, but she wasn't even sparing me a glance—her full attention was on them.

"Uh … sure. Everyone!" I tried to call over the hubbub, but it was almost impossible to get all their attention at once, especially this close to lunch.

"I like your sweater." One of my little cousins ran up to El and gripped his sleeve, running his little fingers over the green detail.

"Thanks." He smiled at him, but the rest of us chuckled at his nervous, deer-in-headlights look—the same one he'd sported at the concert in the park.

That brought Timmy's mom over, and the intros started. Everyone wanted to know who the new guys were, and everyone wanted to catch up with me, since I didn't get to see the extended family that often. I awkwardly introduced the guys as my "friends," not knowing how else to refer to them, but it wasn't long before I was pushed out of the circle and they were doing their own intros to my fascinated family.

The next hour passed in a blur. El, Tin, and Max chatted with my family, played with the kids, and generally delighted everyone.

I helped my mom finish up with lunch, flitting between the kitchen and the living area, completely incapable of keeping my eyes off them or not smiling like a fool every time I made eye contact with one of them.

By the time we all sat down at the long table, which had been set up to stretch out of the dining area and into the living room, three new place settings had been added. The guys were all pulled into seats—none of them near me. I was glad my family seemed to like them, and I was overjoyed at the genuine smiles on the guys' faces, but they were in the same room as me, and I was missing them.

I was seated at the kitchen end of the table near my mom, my aunt, and my cousin Mary.

"So, which one is it, Sadie?" my mom leaned in and stage-whispered. "I feel like you're giving them *all* googly eyes, and I can't figure it out."

"Mom!" I growled. "I do not have googly eyes."

"I don't blame you." Mary laughed. "They're all…" She bit her bottom lip, looking at them as if they were the juiciest turkey. " … delicious."

"Mary!" her mother scolded, but she was my mother's sister, so she laughed at the same time.

I managed to deflect their intrusive questions for most of the meal, but as the table started to clear, Mary shifted over to the seat next to me and leaned in.

"OK, seriously, I need to know which one to keep my hands off. Because they're all hot, but chicks before dicks and all that."

I laughed and gnawed on my bottom lip, looking around to make sure no one was eavesdropping before answering in a low voice, "Keep your hands off all three."

Mary leaned away from me slowly, her eyebrows so high I worried they were at risk of merging with her hairline. My cousin was definitely the wild child of the family, but I was still a bit nervous to tell her I was interested in all three men—let alone that I'd already slept with them.

After a tense moment, her lips slowly pulled into a smile. She crossed her arms and looked me up and down, as if she were seeing me for the first time.

"Good for you." She nodded, and I released the breath I'd been holding, letting myself smile.

Good for me, indeed. It was only hours ago I'd been talking to Dad about taking chances, doing what I really wanted to with my life. Yes, we'd been discussing work, but I was determined to live my life to the fullest in every way. If that included the three elves currently charming my family, I wasn't going to complain.

And in the spirit of going for what I wanted, I stood up and raised my voice. "All right, I'm taking my friends to have an actual conversation now."

"Is that what we're calling it?" Mary mumbled under her breath and took a sip of her wine.

I flashed her a warning look but gestured for El, Tin, and Max to come with me. A chorus of disappointed grumbles went up around the table.

"You just spent half the night with them, pumpkin," my dad complained. "What more do you have to talk about?"

I rolled my eyes at him but turned and walked to the back of the house, knowing the guys were following me.

No one else was in the sunroom, but I still kept my voice down when I turned to them and asked, "OK, what is going on? How is this possible?"

Max rubbed the back of his neck in that adorable way I was coming to realize was a habit of his. "I hope you don't mind us just showing—"

Tin pushed past him, coming straight for me. He enveloped me in a hug so tight he lifted me off the ground. I wrapped my arms around him and breathed him in.

"I missed you." He sighed.

"I missed you too, cutie."

"Dammit," El grumbled, and then he appeared at my back, wrapping his arms around us both. He didn't need to say the words—I knew he'd missed me too.

When they finally set me down, I immediately reached for Max and pulled him in for a kiss. I threaded my fingers through his as I backed away with a massive smile.

"I don't mind you showing up at all, Max. I'm so happy you're here. And my family love you. I just have so many questions."

They all chuckled, and El rolled his eyes. "Of course she has questions."

I smacked him on his rock-hard abs. "Aren't you missing Christmas at the Pole? Surely that's way more epic than my crazy-ass family crammed into my parents' living room."

"Christmas at the Pole is always festive and lively," Max explained with a smile. "It's like our own massive family thing, except there are thousands of us. Festivities start at breakfast when all the sleighs start to roll in empty. But those who may have made connections in the outside world go to see those special people too. We've never had a reason to be anywhere but at the Pole before this year. But we all wanted to spend Christmas with you."

I stared at them for a moment, stunned. "I'm special to you?"

Max blushed, looking sheepish.

El cleared his throat and stepped up. "It's ridiculously early in the rel ... uh ... whatever this is between us. Trust me, I know we only just met last night and this is a little crazy, but we think you could be very special. To all of us. We want to see where this goes."

"We like you a lot, and not just because you jingled all our bells." Tin wiggled his eyebrows, breaking the suddenly intense moment with the perfect joke.

We all laughed, but my heart was bursting. The old Sadie—the one who put up with crap from her ex and worked a dead-end job while pretending she wasn't giving up on her dreams—would've talked herself out of this. She would've argued it was crazy and impractical and downright dangerous to agree to dating three men she'd only just met. But fuck her! These weren't just men—they were elves, and they'd shown me more than one kind of magic that night. I was counting this as my own Christmas miracle.

"I can't wait to get to know you all better." I nodded, a hint of nervousness mixing with the excitement.

"She means she can't wait to ask us a million questions," Max grumbled but with a smile on his face.

"Ask all the questions you want, baby. I love your curiosity." Tin gave me a kiss on the cheek.

"Kiss-ass," El teased, but he looked happy. They all did.

"Presents!" my mother yelled from the living room, her voice carrying over the chatter and through the entire house. The sound of several sets of feet making their way to the tree immediately followed.

"Dammit." I groaned. "The questions will have to wait. Come on."

I rushed into the living room ahead of them. The kids were running around and playing, but the adults were gathering around the tree, chatting, getting ready to open their presents.

"Oh, by the way," I whispered over my shoulder. "Thank you for what you did with my gifts. It means a lot."

"You're welcome." Tin squeezed my hand.

My dad put on a Santa hat, shouted "ho ho ho," and started launching gifts across the room as if he were reliving his quarterback years. Most people caught theirs or managed to call out before he handballed something breakable. One year he did throw a glass jewelry box before my uncle realized what was happening, and my aunt got a box of broken glass that Christmas.

"That's one way to do it." El chuckled.

I nodded. "Yeah, it certainly adds an element of excitement."

My phone buzzed in my pocket. I pulled it out to see a text from Monica.

"I know you love this x-mas shit so merry Christmas. Hope you're having a nice day, wherever you ended up. Love you, ho ... ho ho! LOL! I crack me up."

Smiling, I typed out a quick reply. "Who you calling a ho, skank? I made it home and I'm with the fam. I appreciate the holiday wishes, especially since you want to stab Christmas with a shank. Love you too!"

"Sadie!" Dad called, and I whipped my eyes up just in time to see a brightly wrapped package sailing for my head.

I gasped and squeaked, but a dark hand shot out and caught it inches from my face.

"Watch out!" Max yelled as he saved my life.

A few people cracked up laughing. El shook his head as Max handed me the present, and Tin moved to help my dad—they were throwing gifts at double time with Tin's help, making everyone scramble to catch them all.

Mom appeared behind me and passed me a shortbread cookie, then kissed my cheek with a wink.

My heart was full.

EPILOGUE: THE NORTH POLE

The phone rang as I threw another three T-shirts onto the growing pile on the bed.

"Hello?" I answered it without checking who it was, rushing into the bathroom to look for my hairdryer. I was running out of room in the suitcase, but I wasn't sure if they had hairdryers in the North Pole.

"Are you running or fucking right now?" was how Monica greeted me. "You're out of breath."

"I'm packing."

"I call BS. Packing has never winded me like that."

"It's fucking stressful, OK?" I yelled, then tripped on the pile of boots I was trying to fit into the suitcase and just lowered myself to the floor next to them, defeated.

"Whoa. How about we rein in the bitchy and you tell me what's going on like a normal person. Hmm?" Monica chastised me, but she didn't sound mad at all.

I sighed. "I'm sorry for snapping at you. I'm just nervous about this trip. It's kind of a big deal, and I've been so busy with work I haven't even had time to prepare for it properly. And now we're supposed to leave first thing in the morning, and I have no idea what to take, and I haven't even shaved my legs."

Monica laughed but stopped before I could yell at her for laughing at my anxiety. "OK, let's just take a deep breath. First of all, is everything at work ready? You're set up and good to leave?"

"Yes." I nodded, kicking some boots out of the way and leaning back on the bed. "Joe is all over it. We're managing the start of the holiday rush, and I'll be working remotely over there. It's all set up."

Joe was my business manager and PA, my right-hand man. Three years ago—just after three sinfully sexy elves fell at my feet and took me on a magical Christmas adventure— I'd quit my job at the department store, given notice to my landlord, and moved back in with my parents for six months while I got my lingerie business off the ground. I specialized in unique, high-quality designs that catered to all sizes, ensuring beautiful underwear that was supportive and comfortable. I did limited-edition lines around special dates like Valentines and Christmas. The past two years, they'd sold out.

It had been scary and overwhelming at first, but I'd built the business up from the ground, kept it online only, and now employed twenty staff.

"OK, good. So put that out of your mind." Monica's steady, no-

nonsense voice was making me calmer already. "You can shave your legs in the shower in the morning—that's, like, a five-minute task. All you have to do now is concentrate on the packing. Why is it stressing you out so much?"

"I don't know." I rolled my eyes and leaned my head back on the mattress. "Because it's the fucking North Pole? I mean, I'm going to meet Santa. *The Santa.* I'm nervous and worried I'll fuck it up somehow."

About six months after we started dating, my business was booming, so the guys and I had moved into a spacious apartment halfway between the city and my parents' place. It was fairly close to where I'd set up my office and close enough to my family to visit often. The guys had continued to do their elf duties every year, but I hadn't ridden along since that first time. I'd just meet them at my family Christmas the next day.

The hardest part was when they had to leave for a month. The North Pole took most of the year off—Santa's original Elves were more than capable of managing the place on their own. There was a meeting in January to discuss how the deliveries had gone, then there were planning sessions and catch-ups about once a month, but mostly the Elves and the magic took care of it all.

The recruited elf teams just did the delivering. Most of the time they lived in the real world, but in December, they all went to the Pole for the entire month to prepare, plan, train, hang out with Santa, and do other secret Christmas-magic things I didn't know about.

Being apart for an entire month was hard for us all, so for the first time, they were taking me with them. I was going to the actual

North Pole!

"You're nervous about meeting Santa?" Monica chuckled. "Girl, he's just another old white man. And isn't he supposed to be all jolly and shit?"

I gasped. "He is not just *another old white man*. He is jolly and holly and wonderful. How dare you?"

Despite being let in on the whole "Santa is real" situation, Monica still wasn't a fan of the season. She'd thawed out to the concept and even come to our last family Christmas, but she was still a bit of a Grinch. She and my parents were the only ones who knew. We'd had to get special permission from Mrs. Claus herself to tell them, and even then, it was under a protection spell that prevented them from talking about it to anyone but us. But it made my life easier——I hated lying to people I loved, even if it was a lie that wouldn't hurt them.

"My point exactly!" Monica sounded triumphant. "The man is supposed to be pure joy, the place a magical land of candy canes and shit. No one is going to judge you or make you feel bad. You're overthinking this."

I surveyed the mess around me in silence for a few moments, then a small smile pulled at my lips. I was being ridiculous. "You're right," I grumbled. "I needed to hear that, Monica. Thank you."

"I'm sorry, I didn't quite catch that. Can you repeat it?"

"I said thank you."

"No, the first part."

"You're right," I growled, but it ended on a laugh.

"Ahh. Music to my ears. Now go pack."

"Wait. I totally hijacked that conversation. Why did you call?" I pushed to my feet and headed for the living room. I was pretty sure I'd heard the front door, meaning one of my guys was home, but I'd always make time for Monica.

"I'm in line at the Mexican place. Just called to kill time. Actually, it's my turn next. Gotta go. Bye!"

"Love you too, bitch!" I yelled down the phone as she hung up.

I walked out into the living room just in time to see Tin hanging up his coat and toeing off his boots as he looked around at the mess I'd made. My packing frenzy/freak out was not contained to the bedroom.

"Hey, why is half the kitchen out on the countertops?" he asked with a mixture of amusement and worry.

"Don't worry about that." I wrapped my arms around his neck and leaned in for a kiss. "I've dealt with it now. And it's not half the kitchen. It's just my fave frying pan and the mint hot chocolate mix and a few other things I wasn't sure they'd have at the Pole."

I smoothed Tin's blond hair back, giving him another kiss. During his time in the real world, he was a baker. He came home smelling like bread half the time, but he owned the place, so he wasn't always the one doing the baking.

Before he could respond, the door opened again, and Max walked in.

"Whoa..." He raised his eyebrows at the mess and lowered his messenger bag to the ground.

Max was an operations manager and worked freelance, only taking projects that wouldn't interfere with his North Pole duties. He often had the longest hours, but he also got the most time off in between.

I helped him out of his coat and hugged him from behind, resting my cheek on his broad back. He wore the softest cashmere sweaters.

"Sadie freaked out about the Pole and decided to pack the kitchen sink." Tin moved into the kitchen and started putting everything back in its place.

Max covered my hands on his belly with his and half turned his head to speak to me. "Baby, they have kitchen sinks at the North Pole. They have everything you could possibly need, and if there's something you *can't* find, we can just magic it to you."

I wriggled around to his front and gave him a kiss on the lips. "I know. I'm good now. It was temporary insanity."

He chuckled but helped me straighten up the living area as Tin finished off the kitchen.

I started to pull the curtains shut, then paused at the window, watching through the gap for a few moments. We had an apartment on the fifth floor, and it had great views of the city in the distance. I smiled at the lights twinkling in the steadily falling snow. It had been snowing on and off for about three days, and the park across the road looked like a magical winter wonderland. I loved it at dusk the most, when the light was disappearing and everything kind of glowed.

A pair of hands landed on my hips, and someone pressed his nose to the back of my head and inhaled deeply.

"God, you smell good." El's low voice reverberated through me. I let the curtain fall closed completely, my full focus on him. I'd been so mesmerized by the snow I hadn't even heard him come home.

"That's just because you spend all day inhaling exhaust fumes," I teased. "Everything smells good by comparison."

El loved working with his hands and was a mobile mechanic

with his own truck, appreciating the freedom and independence it provided. He wished he could be around in December to help broken-down people get home during the Christmas season, but he knew the reason he was away at that time was much more important.

"Good point." He dropped his hands and stepped back. "Now that you mention it, you smell terrible."

I turned to face him, and he scrunched his face up before flashing me a grin, making those dimples appear. Between the dimples, the red hair, and the overalls covering his tall frame, he was downright irresistible.

"Rude." I crossed my arms but smirked.

"Can we get pizza for dinner?" Tin asked, coming to stand by us and leaning back against the couch. "Can't be bothered to cook."

"Seconded." Max twisted to face us on the couch, resting his arm next to Tin's hip.

"Done," El and I said at the same time.

"I need a shower first. Someone else order?" El walked off in the direction of our bedroom, and Max picked up the phone.

"Shit!" My eyes widened and I rushed after El, but it was too late.

"What the fuck happened in here?" he called from our room.

The three of us cracked up laughing, but the laughter died in my throat when he appeared at the end of the hallway completely naked. He must've peeled his clothes off as he walked and spotted my mess too late.

He stood with his hands at his hips, every inch of pale skin and toned muscle proudly on display. His hair was a mess and his hands were dirty, but my thoughts were suddenly even dirtier.

"Come on." Tin took my hand and pulled me in El's direction. "Let's have some fun before dinner."

"And then we'll clean up your mess and finish packing," Max added as he appeared behind me, pressing his front to my back. He walked me forward, nuzzling my neck.

El just shrugged, accepting he wasn't going to get an answer now that we'd started *that*, so he turned around and gave me a good view of his tight ass as he led the way into our bedroom.

Tomorrow, we'd get our Christmas on and prove why we all deserved to be on the nice list. But tonight, I was going to do every naughty thing imaginable with the men I loved.

THE END

NOTE FROM THE AUTHOR

Thank you so much for reading *It Started With A Sleigh*! I really hope you enjoyed it and you'll consider leaving a review. And if you didn't like it, that's OK too – I'm always open to feedback.

ACKNOWLEDGEMENTS

First and foremost, thank you to John – my partner in every conceivable way, my pillar of strength, my soft place to land.

Thank you to my friends and family for your continued support and for showing me the fun, exciting, nice things about Christmas during those years when I was in my own retail hell and wanted to stab myself in the eye at the sound of jingle bells or the sight of tinsel.

Massive thank you to my cover designer and editor for your hard work and fast turn-around on this one.

Thank you to Sam, my beta and ARC readers. You are amazing!

Thank you to every single reader who chooses to spend time in the stories I write. You are the greatest gift of all!

And, of course, thank you to Mariah Carey for my fave Christmas song of all time!

ABOUT THE AUTHOR

Kaydence Snow has lived all over the world but ended up settled in Melbourne, Australia. She lives near the beach with her husband and a beagle that has about as much attitude as her human.

She draws inspiration from her own overthinking, sometimes frightening imagination, and everything that makes life interesting — complicated relationships, unexpected twists, new experiences and good food and coffee. Life is not worth living without good food and coffee!

She believes sarcasm is the highest form of wit and has the vocabulary of a highly educated, well-read sailor. When she's not writing, thinking about writing, planning when she can write next, or reading other people's writing, she loves to travel and learn new things.

To keep up to date with Kaydence's latest news and releases sign up to her newsletter here: www.kaydencesnow.com.